DON'T FORGET ME

STACY CLAFLIN

DON'T FORGET ME
AN ALEX MERCER THRILLER #5
by Stacy Claflin
http://www.stacyclaflin.com

Copyright ©2018 Stacy Claflin. All rights reserved.
©Cover Design: Didi Wahyudi
Edited by Staci Troilo

This is a work of fiction. Any resemblance to actual persons living or dead, businesses, events, or locales is purely coincidental or used fictitiously. The author has taken great liberties with locales including the creation of fictional towns.

Reproduction in whole or part of this publication without express written consent is strictly prohibited. Do not upload or distribute anywhere.

This e-book is for your personal enjoyment only. It may not be resold or given away to others. If you would like to share this book with others, please either purchase it for them or direct them to StacyClaflin.com for purchase links. Thank you for respecting the hard work of the author.

Receive free books from the author:
http://stacyclaflin.com/newsletter/

WAITING

The man pressed close against a row of prickly bushes as a pickup truck drove by and then out of sight.

He released a breath. Nobody had seen him. Once he was certain the road was clear, he rose just high enough to see over the plants.

Lights still shone from inside the house.

The man checked the time. Again. He swore.

Something was wrong. The couple was off their schedule. They should've left by now.

But they hadn't.

His heart raced, both with worry and irritation—which would soon turn to anger.

He needed them to leave. Now.

What was he supposed to do? Just keep waiting? Get them out of the house? Find a new location? No! This was the only place that would do. He would have to remain patient.

The problem was that the couple was already late. That meant he had no way of knowing when they would be back, if they did finally leave.

He couldn't do what he needed without the assurance they'd be gone long enough.

The man drew in a deep breath and held it.

One way or another, something had to be done. He couldn't hold onto his treasure for much longer.

She needed to be disposed of.

Now.

This waiting wasn't helping anyone. Least of all him.

He would have to do something.

Wouldn't be the first time he'd had to take matters into his own hands. But it would be trickier. Riskier.

He'd done it before, so he could do it again.

The man pulled out a phone and double-checked it was the burner. Then he triple-checked.

There was no room for errors.

He pulled up the contact list. The few numbers on this phone all showed on the tiny screen. His thumb hovered over the one he needed, ready to tap it.

Slam!

The man jumped, then turned back toward the house.

Two people stood on the front porch. The husband locked the door and turned to his wife. They spoke of a phone call that had made them late.

They hurried to their little sedan and drove off faster than usual.

It was time.

The man breathed another sigh of relief and waited a minute to make sure the couple didn't return.

They didn't.

Frogs bellowed in the distance. Otherwise, everything was silent on the sleepy road.

The other neighbors were either out or settled in for the night. Only the couple who just left were off their schedule.

The man scanned the area, and once he was certain nobody watched, he jumped to his feet and sprinted one block to his car.

He could smell it before he reached it.

He'd waited too long. After this, he'd need to dump the car and get a new one. The smell was too much. There was no way to mask it.

That would have to wait. First, he must bid farewell to his treasure.

How he hated letting go of his sweet prizes. As much as he needed to, it was easier said than done. Each time got harder rather than easier.

Maybe he was getting too old for this.

No! He wasn't.

His treasures were why he got up in the morning. What kept him going each day, whether he had a new one or not.

Tomorrow was a new day. He could focus on a new one then.

For now, he needed to bury his latest treasure.

He held his breath as he climbed into the clunker he'd stolen years ago, and started it. Then he pulled onto the road and drove around the block, parking just out of sight of the back of the now-empty house.

His pulse drummed with excitement. Burying the treasures was always just as thrilling as the rest of the process. A different but equal thrill—part fear of getting caught, part saying goodbye, and part anticipation of the next treasure.

The man looked around the quiet street before climbing out of his car and hefting the oversized suitcase from the trunk. The stench made his eyes water. He gagged and blinked away the tears, then lugged the treasure down the unlit backstreet until he reached the fence.

He easily found the latch on the other side and flipped it over, unlocking the gate. It creaked as it opened—just like it had for years. It was almost as though he were the only one to use it.

Once inside, he quickly closed the gate and looked around the large yard that he had long ago memorized. Everything was the same, except now the garden was expanding. Taking up more of the yard.

Ever since the couple's granddaughter started visiting them, the garden had been getting bigger and bigger.

What he wouldn't do to get *that* little girl and add her to his treasure trove.

He shook his head to clear it, then stared down at the spot he'd picked out just for this special prize.

It was now or never.

The man set down the suitcase and checked his thick gloves. Once he was ready, he found the shovel where it always rested against the house.

He tightened the gloves and got to work digging close to the house, just off to the side of a small garden shed.

The suitcase—his treasure trunk—wasn't very big this time, but he would still need to go deep. The last thing he needed was for the wife or grandchild to decide they wanted to start a new garden here, then find his latest prize.

It was always a risk, given how many of his precious treasures had been buried on the grounds. This newest one was already close to the first one. Maybe they could keep each other company.

That thought offered him solace until he could get his next one.

After a while, sweat broke out on his hairline. He paused and wiped it while catching his breath.

The sound of a car engine made him freeze in place. He listened, waiting for it to drive away.

It didn't.

Instead, it slowed, followed by the squeal of a vehicle's brakes.

It sounded like it was in the front of the house.

They couldn't be home already! This was the night they always left for a solid three hours. Sometimes almost four.

The man leaned the shovel against the shed, crept over to the fence, and peeked over.

He swore under his breath.

They were home early. He knew performing the ritual was a bad idea when the schedule was off.

His skin felt on fire. He ran back over to the suitcase and shoved it into the hole. Only about three inches remained between the top of it and the ground.

There was no time to dig the hole deeper.

A car door slammed, then another.

Conversation.

The man released a barely-audible string of profanities as he filled the hole. He cursed the couple for not giving him enough time to properly say goodbye to his treasure.

Once the hole was filled and the sizable chunk of grass placed back on top, he stared at the leftover dirt. Usually, he took his time carrying it over to the garden.

A light shone from inside. It lit up a good portion of the backyard.

Then it dimmed systematically. Someone was closing the blinds on the sliding door on the back porch.

He glanced back at the pile of dirt. If he took it over to the garden, he would risk being seen. The only thing he could do was to spread it near the shed and hope nobody noticed.

So that was what he did. By the time he had finished, he managed to convince himself it looked just like it had before.

Except that he'd covered grass with the dirt.

It would have to do.

He replaced the shovel as it had been, crept to the corner of the house, and checked the windows. Light shone from half a dozen of them, but they all had the blinds drawn.

With any luck, he could make his escape unnoticed.

But luck was already showing it was not on his side tonight.

He pressed himself against the fence and crept along it toward the gate, managing to stay in the shadows. Then he unlatched the lock and pulled the door.

Creak!

He froze for just a moment before bolting out and closing the gate behind him, not taking the time to check the latch.

Then he ran.

DISCOVERY

Three months later.

"Do you want to plant the rosebushes this morning?" Genevieve Foster took one more sip of her black coffee before setting the mug on the table.

Tinsley only nodded.

Genevieve's chest tightened. She'd really hoped Tinsley would've opened up more by now. Her twelve-year-old foster daughter almost never spoke. Not after the horrors she'd witnessed before coming to Genevieve. The only reason Genevieve could tell the girl was excited was because her eyes were wider than normal as she nodded.

"We'll get to that in just a few minutes." Genevieve smiled. "Want me to make you some more eggs first?"

Tinsley shook her head.

"It's no problem." She waited, hoping her foster daughter might say something, but the fact that she was communicating at all was a good thing. Tinsley communicated with Genevieve, her therapist, a handful of friends, and her foster grandparents—Genevieve's parents.

Although part of the responsibility now lay with Genevieve. Tinsley had started to open up a bit more, but then she'd moved the two of them away from their apartment and friends.

But it was for the best, and Tinsley would start to open up more again. It was all a matter of having patience. And lots of it.

Genevieve emptied her mug, then rose. "I might have another egg. Do you mind?"

Tinsley shook her head.

"Sure you don't want more? I'll already be making some."

The girl again shook her head.

"Okay." Genevieve flashed her a smile, though inwardly she held back a gigantic sigh.

As she fixed herself another fried egg, Genevieve talked about the rosebushes they'd picked up the day before. Though Tinsley didn't respond, she was fairly certain the girl was listening. And according to the therapist, that was important for her overall recovery.

Genevieve continued talking about flowers and gardens until she was done with her breakfast.

Tinsley mostly played with a hangnail.

Having her own demons made it easy for Genevieve to empathize with the girl, although Tinsley had been terrorized from a much younger age. It must've made everything she went through that much harder to deal with. At least, that's what Genevieve told herself to stay positive with her foster daughter.

Before long, the duo was outside with spades and the two rosebushes. The sweet aroma of the buds filled Genevieve with hope that everything would be okay.

It was a stretch, but she was happy to take it. Especially on this notably bright morning in the Evergreen State.

"Do you think the last few days' rain has helped to soften the dirt?"

Tinsley shrugged.

"Let's find out." Genevieve handed her a spade, then retrieved the shovel from the side of the house where her mom always left it. "The guy at the garden center said these have pretty deep roots. How far do you think I should dig?"

Tinsley didn't respond.

Genevieve nodded as though she had. "I think pretty deep, too."

The sun grew hotter with each clump of dirt she dug out. Sweat dripped down her face and stuck to her clothes by the time she was almost done.

One last time.

Clunk!

She and Tinsley exchanged a curious glance.

Tinsley opened her mouth.

Genevieve nearly dropped the shovel in hopes that the girl would speak.

She didn't. Tinsley closed her mouth and stepped closer to the hole.

It took Genevieve a moment to recover, then she struck the hole again.

Clunk!

"Probably just a rock." She forced a smile, knelt, then peeked into the hole. The only rocks were tiny pebbles. Nothing unusual.

She pushed dirt around with the shovel. It scraped along something just below the surface.

Something buried in the garden.

It was probably nothing important. Maybe something a previous resident had buried. When Genevieve was a kid, she'd buried a time capsule in the home she'd grown up in.

Her parents had moved, so this wasn't that house. Some other parent-child pair had probably found her silly box years ago. And perhaps now she and her foster child had found someone else's.

Tinsley nudged her.

"Right. Sorry. Let's see what it is. Maybe a buried treasure."

The girl actually smiled.

Warmth ran through Genevieve. She went back to digging out dirt until she revealed what appeared to be the lid of a fairly large storage container.

Faded writing was scrawled across the top, near the middle. She pushed aside dirt until it was legible.

Halloween decorations.

Why would someone bury those?

She dug around the plastic box, trying to loosen it but grew tired.

Tinsley threw her an impatient glance.

Genevieve took a deep breath and wiped her forehead. "It's going to take a long time to dig this out. Why don't we pull off the lid and see what's inside?"

Tinsley nodded furiously. "Yes."

Genevieve dropped the shovel.

She quickly recovered, then moved the shovel out of the way. With shaky hands, she loosened the two ends of the lid. They were stuck in place, but finally gave way.

Genevieve fell backward from the force.

"Look!" Tinsley pointed in the hole.

She could hardly believe the girl had spoken twice in a row. Her whole body shook as she pulled herself to her feet.

Genevieve peeked down the hole into the storage container.

Inside the box lay two plastic skeletons. Halloween supplies, as the box had indicated.

Except they weren't.

Her heart raced and her entire body shook as she realized they weren't looking at plastic skeletons.

They were real.

Human remains.

Two children, from the looks of it. Wisps of long hair still remained on both. The coloring was dark, unlike fake bones. A hair ribbon stuck out from underneath one skull. Fragments of fabric rested around the two children.

Genevieve couldn't pull her attention from the sight. She needed to do something. Call the authorities. Distract Tinsley.

Keep herself from falling apart.

Her stomach lurched. She ran behind the garden and threw up.

When she came back around, Tinsley was staring at her, wide-eyed.

Genevieve found her voice. "Let's go inside, honey."

"Real? Real?" The girl's voice was high-pitched and her eyes widened. Her mouth gaped open as she looked between her foster mom and the human remains.

"We should go inside and—"

Tinsley screamed at the top of her lungs.

HOPE

Captain Nick Fleshman rubbed his temples as he made his way through the stack of paperwork. "Oh, the glorious job of being a police captain."

A commotion sounded outside his office.

Just the distraction he needed. He blinked his bleary eyes and made his way to the door. The first thing he noticed was what he always noticed when he exited his office.

Genevieve's empty desk. Officially, she was on a sabbatical, though it was anyone's guess if she would actually return to work at the end of the six months.

Nick's guess was no. The fact that she'd cleared her desk, moved from her apartment, and didn't return any of his calls told him all he needed to know.

And it broke his heart. Not that he could dwell on that while at work. Or at home, really. Not as the single dad to three busy kids.

Detective Anderson raced in his direction, his gaze focused on something past Nick.

Nick stopped him. "What's going on?"

Anderson skidded to a stop. "Two DB's found in a backyard."

"Where are the bodies?"

"In town. Want me to keep you updated?"

Nick narrowed his eyes at his friend. "What aren't you telling me?"

Anderson's expression tightened and he looked away. "Officer Foster called it in."

The words felt like a punch to the gut. Nick leaned against his doorframe and nodded toward Genevieve's empty desk with a questioning glance.

"Yeah." Anderson grimaced. "She found the remains in her parents' yard."

Nick struggled to find words. "I'm going with you."

"Captain." Anderson gave him a knowing look. "Do you think that's a good idea?"

Detective Anderson was one of the only people who knew about Nick's relationship with Genevieve. Correction. Nick's former relationship with the officer.

Nick nodded resolutely. "I'm going."

"Okay. I'll ride with you."

The captain grabbed some things from his office before the two headed for his Mustang. Nick followed the line of cruisers speeding away from the station.

Nick's mind raced the entire time. What would he say to Genevieve? What would *she* say to him? Would they only discuss the case and act as though everything was normal when in reality, it couldn't be further from the truth? She'd left without an explanation following some mistakes that made Nick look bad.

He pulled up to the curb behind the precinct's cruisers, then ran toward the cheery yellow house with a distraught older couple on the porch.

Genevieve was nowhere in sight.

The couple led the first officers inside, and Nick waved Anderson in. The air smelled of eggs, bacon, and coffee. Just a normal family, a normal morning—until dead bodies showed up in the backyard.

They followed conversation through the home and out through a sliding glass door.

From the porch, the hole in the ground was easily visible. The bodies weren't.

Nick marched down the steps and made his way around the other officers until he could see inside.

His stomach tightened at the sight of two small skeletons. They couldn't be any older than eight or nine. About the same age as Hanna, his youngest daughter.

It made him sick to his stomach to think of not only what the children had endured, but especially what the parents were going through. They had to have gone missing years ago based on the skeletons, but as a parent, Nick knew that didn't matter. They would be just as heartbroken today as when they discovered their children gone.

He would never forget the terror of finding out his daughter had turned up missing not that long ago. It still felt like yesterday, but he'd been lucky and gotten Ava back alive and well.

Soon the parents of these children would get the worst kind of closure.

Nick stepped away from the chaos and looked around the yard for Genevieve. She was nowhere in sight.

If she'd called this in, she had to be around somewhere. Maybe someone was already questioning her.

He pushed his way through the ever-growing crowd of police and found his way inside.

The older couple—they had to be Genevieve's parents—stood huddled together, watching the scene in their yard.

Nick walked over to them and held out his hand. "I'm Captain Fleshman. Which one of you called this in?"

The woman sniffled and leaned her head against her husband's shoulder. "It wasn't us. It was our daughter. She was digging in the garden—just rosebushes, I swear—when she found... it. Them."

"Do you mind if I talk with your daughter?"

"She's trying to calm Tinsley, her foster daughter. They both saw the skeletons."

Nick nodded. "I understand. Where are they?"

"Past the kitchen, down the hall, last door on the right."

"Thank you." Nick went inside and found the door easily. He knocked.

"Come in," Genevieve called from the other side.

His knees nearly gave out at hearing her voice. He hadn't been sure he ever would again.

Shaking, he twisted the knob. It turned easily, and he pushed the door open.

Genevieve sat on a queen bed, her dark hair was pulled into a ponytail and she wore no makeup. Worry covered her face, but it didn't take away from her beauty. Tinsley leaned against her with an exhausted expression.

Both of their faces registered shock when they saw Nick.

"Nick." Genevieve's voice was barely a whisper.

Tinsley jumped up, pulling away from Genevieve.

Horror ran through Nick as he recalled the last time he'd seen the preteen. She'd ran from him then, too.

But this time, she ran to Nick and threw her arms around him. She had never done that before.

He exchanged a surprised glance with Genevieve before wrapping his arms around Tinsley. "Are you okay, sweetie?"

She shook her head, burying her face into his chest.

Nick rubbed Tinsley's back but kept his gaze on her foster mom. "So, you two found the DB's?"

Genevieve nodded, averting her gaze. "That was the last thing we expected."

"I'm sure it was."

A commotion sounded outside.

"Excuse me." Nick gave Tinsley another quick hug before stepping back and peeking out of the curtain.

A cadaver dog had been brought in, and it was going crazy near a shed.

MORE

Nick raced to the porch and asked the first officer he came to what was going on.

Without looking away from the dog, the officer gestured. "Looks like there's a fresh body."

"Another one? What happened here?" Nick hurried over to the side of the porch and leaned against the railing.

The dog now sat, sniffing the air wildly, while some officers dug near the shed.

The officer holding the leash adjusted it. "She seems to smell something else. I'm going to walk around and see if she finds anything more."

Nobody objected, as nearly everyone was focused on the diggers.

Nick glanced back and forth between the dog and the diggers.

The dog barely made it a dozen feet before indicating she found something else.

"Got something!" The officer pulled out a small flag and stuck it in the spot and took the dog farther. Again, the dog only went a little way before stopping.

"Another one!"

Nick's stomach twisted. What had happened on this property?

Chaos broke out, and for good reason. They had at least five bodies. Maybe more if any of the other graves had two bodies like the first.

Nick went back inside. Anderson and Chang were questioning Genevieve's parents in the living room.

It was going to get a lot worse now that the body count was on the rise.

He went down the hall and found Genevieve and Tinsley still in the bedroom. Tinsley had a novel and didn't look up when Nick came in. Genevieve was at the window. The sight of her took his breath away.

She turned to him, her face pale.

Nick recovered and gave her a sympathetic glance. "How long has your family lived here?"

"Just a few years. Dad wanted something smaller to take care of with all of his health issues."

"I'm sorry to hear that. What problems is he having?"

She glanced back outside. "Typical aging. Aches and pains, early signs of arthritis. That sort of thing. It made taking care of a large two-story harder. They're both a lot happier here. Well, they were. I can't speak to the future. Did they find more bodies out there?"

They stepped as far from Tinsley as possible without leaving the room.

Nick leaned close and spoke in the smallest whisper. "The cadaver dog is going crazy. Nothing new has been dug up."

Genevieve frowned then sighed. "My parents had no idea about any of this. I swear. This place seemed like the perfect place for them to retire."

"I believe you." He sat next to her, leaving a full six inches between them. It wasn't as awkward as he would've expected, given she'd taken off without a word. It was hard not to pull her into his arms. To kiss her like he had that night she'd invited him over. He cleared his throat. "Do you know anything about the previous owner?"

She shook her head. "My parents might. All I know is that a teenager who lived here years ago went missing."

"Really? When was that?"

"Twenty-five or thirty years, I think. Something like that. A cold case. But the skeletons we found are too small to be a teenager."

Nick nodded. "It could be unrelated. Or that girl could be out there, too."

Genevieve frowned, then glanced over at Tinsley, who was furiously turning the pages of her book.

"You might want to prepare for a trip to the station for questioning. Maybe pack some overnight bags. This whole property is going to be a crime scene, and I can't guarantee when you all will be allowed back."

"I know, but thanks." She drew in a deep breath and held it before looking back at Nick.

Their gazes locked, but neither said anything. His pulse raced. He had practically begged her to talk to him the last time they'd seen each other. That might've pushed her away. He needed to be a lot more careful this time.

Last time, it was his family involved in an investigation. Now it was hers. Maybe she would open up to him if he offered support as a friend, and nothing else.

Knock, knock.

Nick pulled away from her gaze.

Anderson stood in the doorway. "Captain, you need to see this."

"What is it?" Nick rose from the bed.

Anderson glanced at Genevieve, then back to Nick. "Come and see."

"Okay." Nick threw her an apologetic glance then mouthed, "Pack your things."

He and Anderson shuffled past other officers to the backyard again.

More than a dozen little flags dotted the yard.

Nick turned to Anderson, his eyes wide. "That many?"

Anderson raked his fingers through his hair. "You haven't seen the ones on the sides of the house."

"There's more?" Nick's mind spun, trying to comprehend the gravity of the situation.

Anderson's expression tightened. "This place is the burial ground of a sick bastard."

"Why this property?"

"It's a big lot."

Nick shook his head. "That's not it. This house means something to the perpetrator. He doesn't live here, yet he returns to bury bodies." He recalled what Genevieve said about one of the previous owners. "Maybe he lived here."

"Could be."

"Foster said about thirty years ago a teenager who lived here went missing. Never found."

They exchanged a serious look.

Anderson wrung his hands together. "Looks like we have another serial killer on our hands. It hasn't even been two years since the last one."

"Two years come Halloween."

"Right. Any chance this is the same guy?"

Nick shook his head. "Flynn Myer dumped them all in bodies of water. Just like his sister had died in a lake."

"I wonder if this guy is trying to recreate something."

"I'm sure we'll find out soon enough."

A voice called from around the house, "Found another one!"

Nick's stomach lurched. He hated that Genevieve was being dragged into the whole ordeal. She and her parents would be persons of interest—there was no doubt about that.

Anderson leaned close and spoke in a whisper. "Do you think Foster's father has anything to do with this?"

"No. He came here to retire and relax."

"Yeah, but it'd make sense if he wanted to retire to where he'd been burying bodies all these years. He could just go into his backyard and visit all those graves."

Nick leaned against the rail. "You'd have to prove that he has ties to this house going back thirty years. Maybe more. I really think they're just at the wrong place at the wrong time. I've certainly been there."

"True, but I'm not leaving any stone unturned."

"What was your feel of him when you questioned them in there?" Nick glanced inside to see Chang still talking with the couple.

"Shocked. Probably never expected to be caught."

"Or maybe he can't believe bodies are buried around his property. That would throw anyone off."

"We'll see. Don't write him off just because… because, uh, we know Foster."

Nick frowned. "I know, I know. Everything by the book."

"Good to hear, sir. I—"

"Another body!" someone called from the side of the house.

"This is a nightmare." Pressure built behind Nick's temples.

Deputy Mackey stepped outside, looked around, then marched over to Nick. "Captain, the media is outside. They want a statement."

"Of course they do."

Anderson glanced at him. "What's the official statement?"

"Some bodies have been found. That's all they need to know for now. I'll handle them." Nick pushed past Anderson and Mackey, then headed for the front door.

NEWS

Alex Mercer took another swig of his double-shot peppermint mocha, hoping it would help him keep his eyes open long enough to get home.

He questioned his sanity for staying in the police academy. Two more guys had bailed this week. Were they the smart ones, or was he?

Alex was in the police academy full time, and he had the option of staying on site in the sleeping quarters. Sometimes he did, but he'd promised Ariana he'd spend some time with her after school, so he was going to keep his word to his daughter.

His exit came into view. Not much farther now. He took another drink of his coffee. Now it was empty. Hopefully, the caffeine would keep him going until he reached his future in-laws' home.

Kenji and Valerie Nakano were Ariana's adoptive parents since Alex and Zoey had been so young when Ariana was born.

Alex pulled off the freeway and fought his heavy eyelids. He blared the radio and sang along with the music, but it turned off and moved to talking.

He was about to switch to a different station when he heard Nick's voice over the speakers. On the radio?

That was enough to wake him up.

Alex listened to his friend carefully, shocked to hear about the possibility of another serial killer in town. Just thinking about it made him drive faster because the last serial killer had taken Ariana from right under Alex's nose just over a year and a half earlier.

She'd been so close to being his next victim.

Alex sped through town, paying close attention to his radar detector. Not surprisingly, there was no activity. With a serial killer just discovered, all resources were clearly focused there.

Time seemed to stand still until he finally made it to the neighborhood he'd grown up in, then to the Nakano house. His tires screeched as he pulled up to the curb and practically flew out of the car.

The door opened before Alex had a chance to ring the bell. Ariana threw her arms around him and squeezed. Alex held her even tighter, relieved to see her alive and well with another serial killer on the loose.

"I missed you so much, but can you let me breathe, Dad?"

Alex released his hold on her, but not completely. "Sorry. I missed you too, angel. I hate being away so much."

"You aren't going to have to work so much when you become a police officer, are you?"

He yawned. "No, I'll actually be here in town. This is more like boot camp, more than fifty miles away."

"How much longer?"

"A couple months, sorry."

"Don't keep him outside," Kenji called from in the house. "He's probably exhausted."

"That I am." Alex stifled another yawn.

Ariana grabbed Alex's arm and pulled him inside. "Come and

see the project I'm working on. It's my end of the year science experiment and is half my grade. Can you believe it? Half!"

Kenji waved from the living room as Ariana pulled Alex toward the stairs, telling him all about her project.

Alex tried to keep up with what she said, but had a hard time, fatigued as he was. He was just glad to see her.

In her room, she pulled out some papers and a magnifying lens. "This is titled Magnifying Power and Focal Length of a Lens." She went on to explain it in more detail, showing him charts and graphs.

It all made Alex's mind spin, but he was sure it'd have made a lot more sense if he hadn't spent six hours in the classroom followed by two hours of physical training. The hardest part was staying awake during lectures. He and his fellow cadets would slap each other when someone nodded off. They had each other's backs—they had to, or they'd never survive.

"Are you listening?" Ariana gave him an accusatory look.

Guilt stung. "I'm sorry, Ari. I swear I'm trying."

"It's okay. Mom, Mimi, and Papi all zone out when I explain it to them, too. And they're not dealing with boot camp. Are we going to go get dinner somewhere, or do you just wanna stay here?"

The thought of going anywhere made every one of his muscles ache even more, but he couldn't say no to her pleading eyes. "I did promise you a meal out."

Ariana clapped. "Thanks, Dad! Can I just fix my hair?"

He kissed the top of her head. She was almost as tall as her mom now. "Sure. I'll meet you in the living room."

Alex plodded down the stairs, half-tempted to lean against the railing and catch a few minutes of sleep there.

Life would be so good once the academy was done.

Downstairs, conversation drifted from the kitchen. Alex forced himself to keep walking.

Zoey and Valerie were at the table, discussing the wedding.

Zoey held up a tablet and was swiping her finger across the screen.

Alex leaned against the doorway and took in her beauty. As always, she was gorgeous. He had known her for his entire life, and somehow Zoey managed to grow more beautiful every day.

And in just over a few months, they would be married. His heart raced at the thought, despite the exhaustion. It was definitely Zoey and Ariana who kept him going through the insanity of the academy. Those two had him wrapped around their little fingers.

Zoey glanced up at him, and her eyes widened. "How long have you been standing there? Some of this is a surprise, you know." She put the tablet face-down on the table.

Alex walked over, cupped her chin, and kissed her, taking in her fruity perfume. "I didn't hear a word. I was too captivated by your beauty."

"Oh, stop." But her grin told him she wanted him to keep going.

He sat in the next seat and scooted closer to her. "It's true. I don't know how I think of anything when you're around. Everyone else pales in comparison to you." Alex glanced at Valerie. "No offense."

The corners of her mouth twitched. "None taken. Excuse me." She smiled at them before heading for the living room.

Alex leaned over and kissed Zoey deeply. He had missed her so much. If only the academy was done with already.

He wrapped his arm around her. She snuggled against him for a minute, then pulled away and went over to the fridge. "Are you hungry? There's some leftover casserole."

"Actually, I promised Ari I'd take her out for dinner. Want to join us?"

"Oh, I don't want to interrupt your daddy-daughter date."

"You won't interrupt anything. Ari's always thrilled when we're all together."

Zoey rested her palm on her stomach for a moment before quickly removing it. "I'm not really hungry."

"Are you sure? We can go anywhere you want."

"Nah. I'm about ready to fall asleep, anyway. Next time you make it this way, we'll all go out for something. Sound good?"

Alex studied her. Something seemed off, but he couldn't put his finger on what, exactly. Maybe it was just him. He had been ready to fall asleep in the middle of the staircase, after all.

Ariana bounced into the kitchen, her hair now in a twisty braid. "Mom! Are you coming with us?"

Zoey kissed Ari's cheek. "Next time, baby doll. I promise."

Ari frowned. "You're both always so tired these days."

"Don't exaggerate." Zoey's eyes widened and she turned to Alex. "Don't listen to her. Work's just been extra busy. That's all. Plus, planning the wedding is more work than I realized. Everything's fine."

Alex put an arm around his fiancée. "Of course it is. Go home and get some rest, and we'll plan dinner in a few days."

"Thanks." She gave him a quick peck, then hugged them both before heading out of the kitchen.

He studied her as she trudged away. Was it just his imagination, or was she actually acting strange?

TARGET

The TV screen flashed back to the police captain, who spoke vaguely about some bodies being found in a backyard.

Breathing heavily, the man twisted his napkin so tightly, his skin caught in it. He threw it on the coffee table and swore.

They knew about his graveyard.

But the question was, how *much* did they know? Had they stumbled upon one of the sets of twins? Or had they found a bunch of the bodies? All of them, even?

This was bad. Very bad. Not only were they going to take his treasures away, but that home would be under surveillance for quite some time.

He wouldn't be able to return to visit his prizes.

They were used to him coming and soothing them. He liked returning to make them feel better, even though they weren't alone. They had each other. He'd given them plenty of others for company underground. But they liked his visits.

It was something he could feel in his bones.

What would he do now? He hadn't given any of his treasures another resting place. They were all together at the house.

The man got up and paced, watching the news coverage. They

either weren't saying much, or they didn't know any more than the police captain had said on camera.

Maybe there was a chance they had only found a handful of the treasures. He could hold onto the hope of returning someday, even if it wouldn't be as soon as he wanted.

It might be time to start anew. He was running out of places to bury his prizes, anyway.

This was clearly a sign, maybe directly from his precious treasures themselves. They were warning him.

They didn't want him to get caught. To get into trouble. They loved him as much as he loved them.

He stopped pacing and flipped through the channels, looking for more coverage. Maybe another station was saying more. He stopped at the first one, but there was nothing new.

He plopped on the couch and checked social media for more information. Everyone was an armchair detective these days. Someone had probably posted findings that weren't being released officially.

But there was nothing other than what the news stations were saying. There were theories flying around, but they were obviously the ramblings of attention-seekers. Nothing more. No truth to any of them.

So far, he was the only one who knew what was really on that property. He intimately knew the stories of each of the girls. Despite the years, the decades, that had passed, no detail escaped him. In fact, he knew them more now than before. He'd relived every glorious moment time and time again in vivid detail.

It was so tempting to post something. To prove to everyone how wrong their pathetic theories were. But that would do no good. He would only out himself and get arrested.

Then what? No more treasures. No more sweet prizes.

No. What he needed was a plan—and to stick with it. His best option would be to follow the case as closely as possible. Maybe even volunteer somehow to see if he could find out what the authorities knew but weren't saying to the public. Keep your enemies close, and all that.

His hands shook. The tremors moved up his arms and throughout his body. His stomach heaved and a wave of desire ran through him.

He hadn't been planning to find his next treasure for a few months, but now with the latest developments, he needed a fix. He couldn't wait that long.

He shook harder, desire pulsating through him like a drum.

Problem was, he needed to be more careful than ever. One misstep, and he'd find himself on death row. The fact that he'd buried all his prizes in the same place meant they could tie him to them all.

If they caught him.

He would have to make sure they never would.

So far, he'd been careful enough not to get caught. Now he would need to be twice as cautious. It wouldn't be long before the cops figured out he found his treasures out of the area and brought them back with him.

Once they made that discovery, they would know to keep an eye out far and wide. Every other city where he'd gotten his prizes would be keeping a lookout, too.

He would either have to go farther away or somewhere new entirely. Going into Canada had been the perfect cover until they tightened the borders. Though he still might be able to get across in the vast woodlands.

No. It wasn't worth the risk. He needed to stay within the bounds of the country.

The tremors grew more intense, until he could hardly breathe.

He needed to find a new prize soon. Now.

Desire twisted and squeezed his insides. He would have to be extra careful, but he didn't have time to put into the pursuit that he usually did—and that was at least half the thrill.

The man went back to his phone and scrolled through random

people on social media. People in the surrounding states who posted public pictures of their kids. Nearby cities. Maybe closer would be better this time since he needed a quick fix.

He saved several who looked like good options and kept searching until he had close to a dozen prospects. Then he narrowed them down to people who had posted photos with the location embedded into them.

That only cut out three from his list.

Next, he narrowed it down further by choosing the ones who posted everything. They would be the easiest to track their schedules.

Three were just outside an area he knew well. If one didn't work, that would leave him with two others in the same general area.

Perfect.

Now it was time to hit the road and find his next treasure.

UNSETTLED

Genevieve stared at her reflection in the two-way mirror. She wasn't used to being in the interrogation room as a person of interest. However, she knew it wouldn't last.

Neither she nor her parents had anything to do with those bodies. Although it didn't look good that some of the bodies appeared to have been buried while they were living there.

But everyone would see it for what it was—some psychopath returning to his favorite location. That's what it was, and the truth would prevail. Why would she or her parents have any ties to the older killings? There was no way to tie them to the newer ones other than the fact that they were buried on the property which, granted, didn't look good on the surface.

They were good, honest people. Hard workers. A lot of people could vouch for them. And she was a cop, for heaven's sake. In this very force. People knew her work ethic. They liked her. Well, Chang didn't, but even he had to know she wasn't a killer.

All anyone would have to do was to see how kids and victims clung to her over other officers, even the other female officers. She was safe. One who upheld the rules. Except she'd slept with the captain. She hadn't just skirted a minor infraction, that was a big one. But look how it turned out—their one-night stand practically shouted, *Sex is bad! Don't do it!*

Genevieve sighed and glanced over at Tinsley, happily reading her novel and blissfully unaware of everything around them. Oh, to be a kid again.

Except a normal kid would probably be freaking out right now. Tinsley had already seen so much, with two now-dead murderers for parents. It was no wonder the poor girl had shut herself away from the rest of the world.

Genevieve's mind flashed back to her own nightmare in the woods, and she shuddered. She was shutting herself away from the world in her own way, by taking her sabbatical. After pushing Nick away—into the arms of his ex-wife, no less—and being forced to face her demons in the woods, she *needed* this break from work.

Not that work was allowing her to stay away. Look where she was—right back in the precinct, sitting in an interrogation room, albeit on the wrong side of the two-way mirror. And now she had to face Nick, too.

And to think, all she'd wanted to do was plant rosebushes to get Tinsley out of the house and into some fresh air.

Why did everything blow up in her face? She couldn't even garden right. Not without it ending up as a crime scene.

Who knew when they'd be allowed back home? Or if her parents would even want to return there after this was all said and done?

At least she had the time to help them move. She had nothing other than time until she returned to work. But even then, she could still transfer to a different department. That would probably be for the best, whether she and Nick worked things out or not. They couldn't be in a relationship with him being her superior, and she doubted she could work under him after everything that had happened.

She stifled a yawn and glanced over at the door. When would

someone come in and talk with her? Were they still grilling her parents? If only she could be with them, but they'd separated the adults. Genevieve had insisted that Tinsley stay with her. Since everyone at the department knew the girl's story, they'd allowed it.

Knock, knock.

The door opened slowly. Nick came in and closed it behind him.

Relief washed through Genevieve at seeing the face of the one she loved, but it was quickly replaced with disappointment. He was the last person she wanted to talk to right now. There were so many personal issues they needed to discuss before *this*.

And that was exactly why she shouldn't have slept with him.

She sighed.

Nick gave her a sympathetic smile. "I'm sorry you two have had to wait so long."

Genevieve tried to ignore the tingles in her stomach. She didn't want to look in his eyes, so her gaze landed on his broad shoulders. Then his kissable lips.

Ugh!

"How are you two holding up?" Nick asked. "Do you need anything to drink?"

"I'm fine." She turned to Tinsley, glad to not have to look at Nick. "Are you thirsty, dear?"

Tinsley shook her head and turned a page in her book.

Genevieve turned back to Nick, but focused on an ear this time. Nothing attractive about ears. Except it looked completely nibble-worthy. She knew that much from experience.

She took a deep breath and stared at a hole in the wall behind him. "How are my parents doing?"

"They're good. Done being questioned. Don't worry, I told both Anderson and Garcia to be gentle with them. We all know you guys are innocent. But questions have to be asked. You know how it goes."

Genevieve nodded. "Are we free to leave?"

"I still need to ask you a few questions. Is it okay with you if I'm in here? Or would you prefer someone else?"

"You're fine." She immediately regretted her choice of words. The man was the finest on the planet, in every sense of the word.

Nick sat down across from her and pulled out a pad of paper and a pen. He turned to Tinsley. "How are you doing?"

Tinsley actually looked up from the novel and met his gaze. She didn't speak, but she was looking at him. That was more than she interacted with anyone else since they'd arrived at the station.

Nick offered her a friendly smile. "I know this is the most boring place on the planet—but don't tell my boss I said that."

Tinsley actually smiled.

"There is a candy machine in the hall. Once I'm done asking Genevieve a few questions about your house, I'll let you pick something out. Does that sound good?"

Tinsley nodded.

Nick glanced over Genevieve. "Is that okay with you?"

"Perfectly."

Tinsley flashed her a smile, then returned to her book.

Nick adjusted his collar, made a note on his paper, then dove into the questions. They were all pretty basic. How long had her parents owned the house? When did Genevieve move in? Had they noticed anything strange about the house or property before today?

She answered them almost without thinking. Her eyes roved over him, offering a pleasant distraction. It made it challenging to pay attention to what he said.

"I'm going to ask about the DB's now. Are you okay with that?" He glanced over at Tinsley. "I can take her to your parents."

Genevieve frowned. "She was with me when we found them. You'll have to ask her the same questions eventually."

His mouth curved down. "She saw them?"

"We were gardening together."

Nick's frown deepened and he glanced over at Tinsley, who was engrossed in her book. "I'm so sorry. After everything she's already been through."

Genevieve nodded. "The good news is that seeing those wasn't nearly as traumatic as what's she has already seen."

"That's one way to look at it. She doesn't seem distraught."

"Not now."

He arched a brow.

Genevieve's heart jumped into her throat. Why did such a simple gesture have to affect her so much?

"Was she upset before?" Nick asked.

Genevieve found her voice. "She screamed when I told her the bones were real. It took me several minutes to calm her down."

He nodded, looking deep in thought, then turned to Tinsley. "Can I ask you about the bones you found?"

Genevieve's chest tightened. She prepared for more screaming.

Tinsley put her bookmark in place, set the book down, and nodded at Nick.

Relief flooded through Genevieve.

The captain kept his voice soft as he asked Tinsley yes or no questions about the skeletons. She kept eye contact with him the entire time and either nodded or shook her head after each question. She didn't yell once. In fact, she seemed calm and at ease.

Genevieve's heart softened as she watched how good Nick was with Tinsley. He wasn't just a good cop, but an excellent father figure—not only to his own kids but also the ones he came across in the line of duty.

More than an hour had flown by when he was done questioning them.

Nick closed his pad of paper. "Does your family have somewhere to stay? I'm not sure when you'll be able to return home."

Genevieve frowned. "I'm not sure. We have some family a few

hours away. Or we can just get a hotel. I'm sure Tinsley would enjoy swimming."

The girl's eyes lit up from behind her book.

Nick scooted back in his chair. "That does sound fun. However, I have another option."

"Oh?" Genevieve leaned forward. "What's that?"

"My condo is in between renters at the moment. Why don't you stay there? It's got some basic furniture—a couple of queen beds, a futon, and a kitchen table. It's nothing fancy, but it won't cost you anything." He glanced over at Tinsley. "And I can bring my kids by. Hanna's been begging me to set up another playdate with you."

Tinsley nodded furiously.

Nick smiled, then turned to Genevieve. "Then it's settled?"

Both he and Tinsley gave her pleading looks. How could she say no? She smiled. "That's really generous of you, Nick. Thank you."

"I'm just glad my condo is available. My renters moved out just a few days ago. They left it sparkling clean."

Genevieve's heart raced at the thought of seeing Nick for a playdate with the kids.

SIGHTING

A lex rubbed his eyes and willed the light to turn green.
It didn't. In fact, it seemed to stay red extra-long just to spite him.

He just wanted to get home and sleep before having to rise early and drive back to the academy before class began. But he needed to stop off at the store real quick for some shampoo. He'd run out the last time he'd stayed at his apartment.

Finally, the light turned green. Alex drove a few blocks before turning at the first convenience store.

He stumbled inside, so tired he probably looked drunk. Now it made sense why he'd heard that driving while tired was as dangerous as driving drunk. He could barely think straight. But at least he'd still remember this in the morning.

Once he found the shampoo, he picked the one Zoey liked the smell of then headed for the register.

He froze halfway down the magazine aisle.

Flynn Myer.

The man who abducted Ariana. Who had taunted Alex. The man who was supposed to be in the Washington State Penitentiary, awaiting execution halfway across the state. Nick had checked every other time Alex had seen Flynn.

Yet there he was. Walking around as a free man.

It made no sense. He had changed his appearance, but he was the dangerous criminal. There was no doubt about that. His hair was now longer and wavy instead of short and thinning. He now had bright blue eyes. He was also tan instead of a pasty white complexion. All were easy enough to change.

Alex's fatigue melted away. Anger and determination ran through him.

Flynn was just staring at bags of potato chips like he hadn't done anything wrong.

Furious, Alex marched over to him. "Are you following me?"

Flynn jumped a little, then turned to Alex. Recognition flickered across his face. Just like it had at the school not that long ago. His eyes widened with surprise.

He wasn't expecting to see Alex.

An interesting twist.

Alex clenched his fists. "I said, are you following me?"

Flynn stood straight. He didn't respond. The weasel never did. All he ever did was run. Would he again? Flee out of the store like the criminal he was?

"What were you doing at the middle school? Looking for your next victim?" Alex stepped closer. He prepared himself to block Flynn's fist. "Does it make you feel like a big, tough man going after little girls?"

Flynn's brows drew together. "I'm not who you think I am. And no, I'm not following you. Just like I wasn't when your daughter was missing."

"Then you *are* Flynn!"

His eyes darted around before landing back on Alex. "Like I said, I'm not who you think I am. Flynn is in prison. Give them a call."

"Oh, I know someone is in prison, disguised as you. I don't know how you did it, but you evaded your sentence."

Flynn laughed.

How dare he actually laugh about that? Alex gritted his teeth, barely able to keep himself from punching him to a pulp. "You have balls, you know that?"

"You bet I do. Leave me alone before *you* end up in jail again."

Alex gave him a double-take.

"I'm serious." Flynn grabbed a bag of ranch-flavored chips. "Stay away from me, or you're going to regret it. I'm not who you think I am. Remember that."

They stared each other down for a moment before Flynn grabbed another bag and stormed to the cashier.

Alex stood there, dumbfounded. As tempted as he was to make a scene, he knew it wouldn't do him any good. It never had—he either ended up in an interrogation room, or like Flynn said, in jail. That had only been one time, and it had been taken off his record, but still it had happened.

And Flynn knew about it.

Alex's blood boiled as he watched the criminal walk out the door. He hurried down the aisle to look outside and see what car he was driving. Maybe even get a license plate or a photo. Something to prove that Flynn was actually walking around free. And if that didn't work, there was also the video surveillance the store had to have.

By the time Alex reached the window, Flynn was already out of sight. His pulse drummed in his ears as he scanned the dim parking lot.

The coward was probably hiding.

"Do you need something?"

Alex turned toward the cashier. "Uh, yeah. Just this." He went over to the counter and handed her the shampoo bottle, but kept his attention on the parking lot.

He muttered a thanks as he left. Once outside, he studied every car in the lot for someone who might be hiding. Then he walked around, just in case Flynn was cowering behind a tree or trashcan.

He wasn't.

Despondent, Alex headed for his own car. On the bright side, he was no longer struggling to stay awake.

As he drove home, his mind raced. He clenched the steering wheel so tightly, his knuckles turned white.

It was hard to believe he kept running into Flynn on accident. It couldn't be a coincidence. Sure, their town was pretty small but it wasn't tiny.

And what did he mean by, *I'm not who you think I am?*

Who else would he be? He'd obviously managed to get someone to take his place in prison.

The man had connections. That much was obvious. How else would he be able to get away with that? He would also need to create a whole new identity with Flynn Myer being in Walla Walla. He'd need more than just a different look, he'd have to get a new home and job. Bank account. Car. Everything would have to be replaced.

Alex pulled into his apartment complex and parked but didn't get out. He needed answers.

SECRETS

Zoey pushed the cans into the shelf, closed the cabinet door, then went into the living room. "Do you need anything else?"

Genevieve's mom flashed her a grateful smile. "No, you've already done plenty. You didn't need to bring over all this stuff."

Zoey leaned against the wall of Nick's condo and stifled a yawn. "You've been displaced from your home. It's the least I could do for a friend." She smiled at Genevieve. "I can come by with Ariana on Saturday. She's missed Tinsley."

Tinsley looked up at the mention of her name. She smiled shyly at Zoey, who gave her a friendly smile in return.

They agreed upon the details of the playdate, then Zoey headed for the door. She shook everyone's hands. "It was a pleasure to meet you, Mr. and Mrs. Foster."

Genevieve's mom squeezed her hand. "Brenda, please."

"And Walter," Mr. Foster chimed in.

Zoey nodded. "Brenda and Walter, it was a pleasure. Let me know if you need anything else. I'm serious."

"You've already done plenty, but thank you."

After the adults all thanked Zoey yet again, she made her way outside into the cool night. She drew in a deep breath and headed for her turquoise electric car.

Halfway there, her stomach lurched.

No. Not now. Not here.

It lurched again, this time with more force.

Zoey looked around, and her gaze landed on a bush. That would have to do. She ran over and threw up just behind it.

The sight of her vomit made her spew again.

She stepped back, leaned against a tree, and wiped her watery eyes. The all-day sickness should've been gone by now. Or at least it had been when she'd been pregnant with Ariana. Hadn't it? Thirteen years was a long time to remember a detail like that.

Zoey rubbed her rounding belly. She was certain her stomach was growing faster this time. From what she'd read, that was normal. She was already wearing loose shirts and using a rubber band to loop around her pants' buttons.

That meant it would be all the harder to keep it from Alex. She'd wanted to wait longer before bringing it up to him. Partly hoping she might miscarry—as horrible as that was. It was her baby in there, but it wasn't Alex's. The father was a crazed lunatic who had shot up a school, held Zoey captive, then raped her before letting her go, probably thinking she was dead.

Tears blurred her vision. She hadn't spoken a word of Dave's last assault on her since she'd been at the hospital and had to share every last detail with the staff. The examination had felt like another attack, even though the nurses couldn't have been nicer.

The whole world would know about it when Dave finally had his trial. She would have to give her testimony.

That would be easier than telling Alex. Her heart felt like it would explode out of her chest just thinking about *that* conversation.

They were planning their wedding. They had big dreams of having a family together. Of giving Ariana siblings. Not half-psychotic siblings. What if her baby ended up as crazy as Dave and his kid? Was the kid nuts because Dave raised him or because of genetics?

And the biggest questions of all—would Alex still want her after what Dave had done to her? And could he accept this baby? One that didn't belong to him?

Tears spilled onto her cheeks. She wiped them away, then covered her vomit with loose dirt before trudging to her car.

One thing was certain. She would have to tell Alex soon. Especially given the chance that all her wedding plans were for nothing if he couldn't accept her pregnancy.

STALK

The man rolled over and pulled stale, stiff blankets over his head. Nothing worse than cheap motel bedding. Except maybe the quality of his sleep over the last several hours. Or at least that's what it felt like—hardly any sleep.

His phone beeped again. This time, he realized it wasn't the alarm.

It was a notification. One of the families he was watching must have posted an update.

Excitement drummed through him. He was getting closer to his next treasure.

He threw off the blankets and sat up, reaching for his phone on the nightstand.

It wasn't just one notification. He'd slept through some others while tossing and turning on the rock-hard bed.

There were half a dozen new notifications.

Hardly able to breathe, he unlocked the screen with his thumbprint and scrolled through the new pictures. Two of the parents had posted morning updates of their daughters.

A little blonde girl grinned widely, showing a recently-lost tooth, as she sat behind a pile of pancakes with a tower of whipped cream covered in sprinkles. The photo's caption read, *Happy Birthday, Maisie! You're the best! XOXO*

So, it was her birthday. All the better. He loved showering his beloved prizes with gifts. This would give him the perfect excuse. Not only that, but with today being her birthday, it would be even more of a challenge to capture her. All eyes would be on her.

The man's pulse drummed in his ears. Up until this moment, he hadn't been sure which one of the three would be his prize, but now he had his answer.

Maisie.

She even had a beautiful name to go along with her angelic face. The name was old-fashioned but at the same time had a modern ring to it. Like it might be topping all the name charts soon.

He scrolled through Maisie's mom's public feed again until he found the pictures of her school. Parents these days made it so easy. She had first day of school pictures—ten of them to be exact—right next to the school's sign. Back before social media, he'd had to work a lot harder on the lead-up to the nabbing.

That part itself was still a wild thrill and always the most challenging part of the process. Each kid was different. Some responded to presents and candy despite their parents' best efforts to teach stranger danger. Others needed befriending. Days of work before everything paid off.

What would Maisie like? He would start with something for her birthday. A pink balloon maybe. Perhaps even a whole bundle of them.

Beads of sweat broke out around his hairline. He might have his next treasure before dinnertime.

CLUE

Nick rubbed his temples and downed the rest of his stale coffee. He fought a yawn, but it won. With as little sleep as he'd gotten the night before, he would be yawning all day. He might have to take a catnap on the couch in his office.

Right then sounded good, but he'd just gotten to the office within the hour. And besides, people kept coming in with questions or new information.

Knock, knock.

Right on cue.

Nick glanced through the blinds at Detective Garcia and waved him in.

The detective entered and sat on the other side of Nick's desk, talking a mile a minute. He was exhausted, too. His accent became more defined during the tougher cases.

"Slow down." Nick put his hand out. "Did you say they found even more bodies?"

Garcia nodded. "We're up to almost thirty. Thirty!"

"What's the actual number?"

"Twenty-eight."

DON'T FORGET ME

Nick's stomach twisted. "Whoever this guy is, he's up there with some of the state's most notorious serial killers."

"Especially if this isn't his only burial ground. If he has another property or two…"

Both men shared a disturbed glance.

"How much of the property has been dug up?" Nick asked.

"Most of it, and they're still going. Can't rely on the dogs for a lot of the older ones."

Nick flipped through some of his notes. "The oldest ones are estimated to be about thirty years old?"

"I'm no bone expert, but that's what it looks like. We're waiting on official word, and everything's being taken to Seattle."

Nick raked his fingers through his hair. "We need to consider sending some of the remains elsewhere. It's going to take them forever to get through all that. Plus, they're sure to have plenty of their own cases to work on."

Garcia nodded. "At least this case is top priority. With so many victims attributed to one guy."

"What about the media circus outside?" Nick had seen a crowd out front when he'd arrived at the station. He parked in the back where the vultures weren't allowed, so he'd been able to avoid them.

"It's getting worse. News is spreading far and wide. There are camera crews from the east coast and even Canada. Chang got some calls from Australia and London earlier. We're famous."

Nick groaned. "I already am."

Garcia lifted an eyebrow.

"When I took the kids to the Seattle Center recently, a twentysomething stopped me near that big fountain and wanted a selfie with me. He recognized me because of how many times I've been interviewed on the news. It's crazy, especially given the size of this town."

"Seriously?"

Nick nodded.

"I never would've guessed. When I applied here, I thought this was a sleepy little town. Nice quiet place to start my career until I settled into the job."

Both men burst out laughing. Between all the abductions and killings, their police force was double other towns twice their size.

Garcia unbuttoned his top button and leaned back in the chair. "What do you think it is about this place? What draws all the crazies?"

"I'm not sure I want to know."

They discussed theories for a few minutes before Garcia went back out to deal with some calls.

Nick dealt with a few pressing emails before walking around the office and stretching. As much as he hated having another serial killer on their hands, he was grateful it had brought Genevieve back into his life.

Ever since she'd left on her sabbatical, he'd been trying to find her without any luck.

Now she was staying in his condo and had agreed to a playdate with the kids. If Nick could get away early today, he'd take the kids over after school. Maybe he could even talk her into letting him treat her and Tinsley to a movie to get everyone's minds off everything. It was Friday night, so nobody would have to get up early the next morning.

Except maybe Nick. It was already an all-hands-on-deck case, which meant there were no excuses. Be there or risk your job.

It was nice to be on the case after not being allowed on the last two big ones, since he was close to the victims. Once the Fosters were cleared as persons of interest, Nick had nothing to do with this case or anyone involved, other than that Genevieve and Tinsley had dug up the first two bodies.

He stopped pacing, and glanced out the window. Everyone was busy, either typing furiously on a laptop, talking on the phone, or running from one place to another.

Which reminded him to get back to work. Between the stack of papers on his desk and the unusually high number of unanswered emails, he had enough to keep him busy for weeks—even if he stayed at the office and didn't sleep the entire time.

Nick glanced over at Genevieve's empty desk and sighed. Would she return to the force? Or was she thinking about working on a different force so they could pursue a relationship?

His chest tightened. Genevieve was the only one he'd given his heart to other than his ex-wife—the woman who would now be spending the rest of her life behind bars due to her part in hiding a kidnapper. He didn't like to admit he was glad to not have to deal with her any longer, especially given how hard she'd made it for him to see his kids. But he did hate how her incarceration hurt them.

They were all in therapy to deal with it. There was only so much Nick could do to help them through something so traumatic. His parents were still married and living a quiet life, so he had no way to relate to what his kids were going through.

"Focus on the case, Fleshman," he muttered to himself. Once he clocked out, he could worry about his kids and love life.

Nick opened his door and headed straight for the coffee pot.

A woman about his mom's age was just closing the lid. She smiled at him. "Fresh coffee..." She glanced at his badge. "...Captain."

"Wonderful. Thank you." At least it would be hot. He poured some into a cup, then introduced himself.

She smiled warmly. "I'm Mary. Just started today."

Nick raised the hot drink to his lips then froze mid-sip.

Mary's eyes widened. "Is everything okay, Captain?"

He lifted the cup into the air. "This is the best cup of coffee I've ever had here! Someone give Mary a fat raise!"

A few people chuckled, but even more raced over to try the drink. Officer Grant declared her Queen of the Snack Table.

It was the perfect distraction from the stress of the case, but unfortunately it only lasted a few minutes before everyone dispersed.

Nick opened his door when someone called out his name.

"Captain! You have to see this."

"What is it?" Nick turned to see Detective Anderson. His expression was solemn.

Anderson gestured to Nick's office. They went inside and sat on either side of the large mahogany desk.

Nick waited. It was obvious by the look on the detective's face the news wasn't good.

"We have an ID on one of the bodies."

"That's good news." Nick breathed a sigh of relief. Maybe he'd misread Anderson.

His expression was still dark. "A teenage girl. Thirty-two years ago. Dental records confirmed her identity. Amy Michaels."

"Go on." Nick's stomach tightened, waiting for the bad news.

"She was reported missing from the house where we found all the bodies."

Nick nodded, taking in the news. That wasn't altogether surprising since a girl living there had gone missing around that time. "Okay, so what's the problem?"

Anderson took a deep breath and paused. "Her father worked with Walter Foster at the time."

Everything spun around Nick as he tried to make sense of the news. "Come again?"

"Nick, the dead girl is connected to Genevieve's father."

MISSING

The sounds of screaming woke Genevieve from a deep sleep. She jumped from the futon and ran into the bedroom where Tinsley was sleeping. Her heart pounded like a jackhammer.

The girl was hollering, but still asleep.

Genevieve sat on the bed and put her hands on Tinsley's shoulders. "Wake up! It's only a dream."

She kept thrashing around and crying out.

Genevieve's mom appeared in the doorway. "What's going on?"

"Tinsley's having another nightmare." Genevieve helped Tinsley to sit up. "Wake up!"

The girl's eyes flew open. She gasped for air. Her eyes darted around before she relaxed in Genevieve's hold.

"Everything's okay." Genevieve's mom sat down and rubbed Tinsley's back. "We're both here, and we're safe in the police captain's condo."

Tinsley took a deep breath but didn't say anything.

"What was your dream about?" Genevieve asked, not that she expected a reply.

"Bones."

She stared at Tinsley. On one hand, it was progress that she answered, but it also made her sick that the girl was now further traumatized by the events of the previous day.

They would never be able to return to that house without the memory of what they'd seen. And her parents would never be able to sell it after this. It was all over the news.

Genevieve pulled Tinsley close. "It's all going to be okay. You're safe, and we're here to protect you."

"Hungry." Tinsley pulled back.

Two words in a row?

Her mom jumped up. "I'll make something. Zoey brought over some eggs. How does that sound?"

Tinsley nodded.

They all went to the kitchen. Her mom twisted open the blinds and bright sunlight assaulted their eyes.

Genevieve covered her face. "Why is it so bright?"

"It's nearly noon, dear." Her mom opened the fridge.

"I don't know why that surprises me. We got to sleep so late." She poured a glass of milk for Tinsley. "Hey, where's Dad?"

Her mom shrugged.

"You don't know?"

"No. He was gone when I woke in the middle of the night to use the bathroom. You know how he is when he gets stressed. Takes off to think."

Genevieve did the mental math. "How long has he been missing?"

"I'd hardly call it missing." She dropped a chunk of butter onto a pan, making it sizzle. "I knew he needed some space to think when he insisted on going out to buy snacks last night. I'd hoped he'd feel better, but he seemed kind of spooked when he got back, don't you think?"

Genevieve shrugged. "We're all on edge."

Her mom pushed the butter around with a spatula. "He was.

That's why I wasn't surprised to find him gone last night. He'll be back soon enough. Just needs some time to process everything."

Genevieve didn't respond. Now was the worst time for him to take off. It could make him look guilty. They had nothing to hide, but he was giving the police reason to suspect him by taking off like that in the middle of an investigation. Hopefully, he'd be smart enough to return soon. If they were asked to go into the station for more questioning, the officers would have reason to think he was hiding something.

"Would you make some coffee, hon?" her mom asked.

"Yeah, sure." Genevieve poured Tinsley some more milk, then poured ground coffee into the machine and added water. "I'm going to call Dad."

"I already tried. He's not answering."

She gritted her teeth. "Maybe he will this time."

"Probably went fishing at his favorite spot. It's out of cell range." Her mom cracked an egg and scrambled it.

"Why would he do that? The police haven't cleared us!"

"We're innocent. Everyone knows that. We've only lived there for a short time, and clearly" —she glanced at Tinsley— "the *activities* have been going on much longer than that."

"But still, under your noses! Some of those were definitely buried there within that time period."

Her mom glanced at Tinsley and back to Genevieve. "Let's not discuss this now."

She clenched her fists. "We have to be careful, that's all I'm saying. If they call us back to the station, it's going to *look* bad if we don't know where he is. It doesn't matter what the reality is."

"Innocent until proven guilty. We've done nothing wrong."

"It isn't that simple." Genevieve stormed out of the kitchen before the conversation ended up heated. She grabbed her purse and pulled out her phone to call her dad.

She had two missed calls from Nick. From his work number.

They *had* to want them to come in for more questioning. There was no other explanation. And her dad was missing.

Unless Nick was only calling to check on them. Maybe that was it.

Either way, she needed to talk with her dad before returning Nick's calls. No way could she call him not knowing where her dad went.

Genevieve grumbled under her breath as she called her dad. It rang five times before going to voicemail. She called three more times before leaving a message for him to come back right away before he ended up looking guilty for something he hadn't done.

Then she called him one more time for good measure. Not surprisingly, it went to voicemail.

She sent him a text telling him the same thing she'd said in the message.

Hopefully, he would heed her advice. The last thing anyone needed was for the police to look at him as a suspect. It would waste the time of the force, focusing on an innocent man, and add a lot of unnecessary stress to the entire family.

Genevieve checked for missed voicemails. There were none.

Maybe Nick was only calling to check in since he hadn't bothered to leave a message or a text.

Her phone rang.

It was Nick.

WAVERING

Zoey turned into the parking lot and saw Macy's car right away. She pulled in next to it then hurried inside the restaurant.

Macy sat on a bench near the door, rocking the baby's car seat and speaking to an elderly woman next to her.

A calmness washed over Zoey, seeing her lifelong best friend and future sister-in-law. They were more like sisters anyway, so marrying Alex would only make their sisterhood official.

She stood by the door for a couple minutes until the person sitting on the other side of Macy was called. Zoey sat, and only then realized how much her legs ached. Almost everything did, and what didn't was bathed in fatigue.

This pregnancy was far harder on her than when she was carrying Ariana. Because she was older? Or because of everything she'd gone through, including the weight of keeping all this to herself?

"Zoey!" Macy smiled widely. "How long have you been here?"

"Just sat down, actually." She covered her mouth and yawned.

Macy patted Zoey's knee. "You okay, Zo?"

That was a loaded question, especially coming from her best friend, who she couldn't give a pat answer to. "I'm getting by."

Macy's smile faded. "Have you gone back to the counselor to talk about your abduction?"

Zoey frowned. "I don't need a shrink. I talked to the one they recommended at the hospital. She was nice and everything, but it just wasn't for me."

"It's not like that. Some things are just too big to deal with on our own. You're always welcome to talk about what happened with me, you know. We've both been through more than most people triple our age."

Tears stung Zoey's eyes. "I just don't want to think about it. Any of it."

"Macy!" A server with short magenta hair and matching lipstick looked around the crowded waiting area.

Macy squeezed Zoey's knee and rose. "That's us."

The server glanced at the car seat. "Do you want a baby seat cradle?"

"That'd be great, thanks."

They got situated at the table, and somehow little Caden Alexander slept through everything. With his car seat nestled into the cradle, they could watch him almost at eye level. He made a cooing noise and smiled, still asleep. Oh, to be that carefree.

Zoey and Macy made small talk as they flipped through the menus. Hardly anything looked good to Zoey, and every image with chicken caused her stomach to lurch. She decided on soup and salad—the only thing that sounded remotely good.

After they ordered, Macy turned to her. "I'm serious about talking, Zo. Call me day or night. I'll probably be up, anyway." She glanced over at baby Caden and smiled.

"Thanks." Zoey tried to imagine what it would be like for her when she had a baby again. Would she be alone? Would Alex or her parents be there for her? What would everyone think of her when they found out what Dave had done to her? Would they pity her? Think less of her? Tears threatened again.

Macy frowned. "You look like you have the weight of the world on your shoulders."

Zoey hated being weak. She hated everything Dave had done to her from the moment he took her at gunpoint to his final and lasting assault on her. The only thing that gave her any peace was knowing she had fought back and gotten away. He hadn't killed her. He hadn't won.

"If you have time, we can walk around the park down the block after we eat. It's usually pretty quiet there." Macy gave her a sad smile.

Zoey nodded. She didn't feel like going back to work, so she may as well get some fresh air and sunlight with her friend. Perhaps they could walk in silence, or Zoey might talk. Not about the pregnancy, but maybe the abduction. Maybe. "I'd like that."

Macy yawned, then rubbed her eyes. "We're quite the pair, aren't we? We both need naps."

Zoey cracked a small smile. "Isn't that the truth?"

The waiter dropped off the food, and Zoey was spared from needing to talk just yet. And luckily, Macy didn't notice Zoey picking at her food. The soup and salad were both delicious, but her stomach didn't want anything to do with either.

A half hour later, they were walking around the park with the now-awake Caden wrapped to Macy's chest.

They followed the trail to a flower garden, where the only sounds were from the birds and children playing at the other end of the park.

Macy fussed with Caden, giving Zoey the chance to stay quiet. Not that she felt better about not having to talk. A big part of her wanted to tell everything to Macy—there was little the two kept from each other.

At last, Caden settled down. Macy stopped at some pretty purple lilies and took a deep breath. They strolled around, smelling the wide variety of flowers in silence. The sun was warm and comforting.

They reached a bench and Macy sat.

Zoey hesitated. This was it. No more putting off the inevitable. Even just talking about the abduction part of her ordeal would likely bring her tears.

"I won't bite." Macy smiled and patted the seat next to her.

Zoey swallowed, then sat. Speaking with a counselor didn't seem so bad. It might be easier to open up to a stranger.

Macy slid her sunglasses to the top of her head and glanced over at some tulips. "You know what I think the worst part of being abducted is?"

"What?"

"Being helpless. Aside from the abuse, obviously. Being unable to stand up for myself. Saying no, but being ignored. There's nothing worse than having our personal boundaries violated." Macy drew in a deep breath and held it a moment. "It's dehumanizing."

Zoey choked on air. Tears blurred her vision. Everything closed in on her. She struggled to breathe and blinked the tears away.

"But you know what?" Macy turned to her, meeting her gaze.

Zoey closed her eyes and shook her head no. It didn't help her to feel less suffocated.

"We're overcomers, you and me. We made it through everything alive. They can't get to us anymore. We're going to live productive lives while they rot in jail, never to walk freely in a park like we are."

Zoey didn't respond. She just wanted the whole world to disappear and leave her alone. She squeezed her eyes tighter, refusing to open them.

Macy's hand slid around hers. "If you'd like *me* to be your counselor, I can. I'll give you patient confidentiality. Nothing you say will go beyond us. Not that it would, anyway."

Zoey opened her eyes. Even though she knew Macy was a counselor, she often forgot. To her, Macy was just her friend. The girl she'd grown up with next door and vacationed with more than her own parents.

"Whatever you want to do, I'm here for you." Macy squeezed her hand.

It seemed to take forever, but Zoey finally looked her friend in the eye.

Could she voice the truth?

WATCHING

The man lowered his sunglasses just enough to peek over the top of them. It was hard to see around the bushes, but at least his car was hidden.

Across the street, the school looked more like a ghost town than a place full of kids. There was no activity, save the occasional adult coming and going.

He glanced at his watch. Only ten more minutes before the recess bell would ring. A chill of excitement ran through him from head to toe.

It would be easy enough to get to the playground. The fence would hardly be a deterrent. The real challenge would be getting Maisie alone. Away from all the kids and teachers. Luckily, the buildings offered plenty of places to hide.

He glanced back at the pink balloons bobbing around in the backseat. The question was whether to bring one with him. It would only draw attention to himself. And what he needed was to blend in. Give no reason for anyone to raise an eyebrow.

The promise of the balloons and a pretty wrapped present should be enough to make the girl come with him. Kids were far more interested in shiny presents and treats than following their parents' advice. Kids were stupid like that.

That was exactly why he had both—if the gift and balloons didn't work, he also had candy. Lots of it.

He checked the time again. Six minutes.

His heart leaped into his throat. The thrill of this part never dulled.

The phone rang. He jumped and gripped the steering wheel.

Why hadn't he silenced it yet? The stupid thing had been going off all morning.

He picked it up to turn off the ringer when the screen showed it was Gayle, his girlfriend. She had the worst timing. Always.

If he answered, she'd stop calling. Hopefully. He could say hi, then end the call and still get across the street in time to blend in with the mass of people heading to the playground once the bell rang.

He accepted the call. "I told you I'd call when I could."

"Why have you been avoiding my calls, Tony?"

"I've been busy."

"Do you think I've been calling for nothing?" Gayle demanded.

He squeezed his fists. "And you know I need to focus when I'm traveling."

"Am I even important to you?"

"Not this again. I keep telling you, yes!"

She sighed into the phone. "Then why are you always gone? Avoiding me?"

"I'm not avoiding you!" Though he was beginning to wish he had.

"You know what? If we're going to be together, you have to pay me more attention! There are plenty of guys who would be happy—thrilled, even—to be my boyfriend. You don't seem to care. That needs to change. Now."

He clenched his jaw and glanced at the time.

Two minutes before the bell.

Time to end the call.

"Are you there? Don't you ignore me, Tony!"

"We can talk about this later," he said through gritted teeth. "When I'm back in town."

"No."

"No?" Had he heard her correctly?

One minute before the bell.

"You heard me. I'm sick of this. I feel more like a mistress than your girlfriend. Tell your boss you need some personal time. Demand to work less hours. Be a man!"

Fury ran through him. "I *am* a man, Gayle! You need to back off."

"I'm the only one you have the balls to stand up to. You give into everyone else. And you know what? I'm sick of it. Things are changing, and they're changing now. One way or another."

"Are you threatening me?"

The bell rang.

He clenched his fists.

"I'm giving you an ultimatum," she said. "It's not a threat."

Kids poured out of the school, filling the schoolyard. He should've been there. Already making his way toward Maisie.

"Tony? Are you there?"

"We'll talk about this when I get back."

"No. We're talking now. Will you stand up to your boss, or are we through? I need an answer. Now."

"I said we'll talk later. I have to go."

The line went dead.

He looked at the screen. It showed the call ended.

Swearing, he chucked the phone across the car. Now he was in no state of mind to head across the street. He would have to wait for the last recess of the day. Maybe pick-up time, but most schools had strict regulations about who the kids went with these days. These things were so much easier back in the day. Nobody ever let kids out of their sight anymore. Helicopter-parent sissies. Pansies—the whole lot of them. A whole society of ninnies.

And what was it with women these days? Always thinking they could order him around. Go here, do that, don't do this. Blah, blah, blah. Emotional castrators, that's what women were. Worthless, stupid, and infuriating emotional castrators.

He squeezed the steering wheel until his knuckles turned white then glanced over at the playground full of kids. *They* weren't controlling. *They* weren't cruel or patronizing.

Kids were kind and accepting, full of grace. Until they hit a certain age and turned into jerks. They always did. It was like a phase of life nobody missed. Especially the girls. They all turned into women at some point.

He shuddered at the thought.

If only the sweet little girls could stay that way. But they never did.

He turned his attention back to the school, and he watched the teachers. They were the ones he'd have to be careful about when the kids came out for their next recess. There were only three of them from what he could tell. Definitely not enough to watch all the kids at once. Especially not with one of the teachers glued to her phone.

Maybe bringing Maisie back to his car wouldn't be so difficult after all.

He would only have to wait for the next recess.

SUSPECT

Nick paced his office. Genevieve probably had a good reason for not answering his calls. Maybe she was sleeping. He could understand that. If he could take a nap, he'd crash on his couch in a heartbeat.

Now there was no time for that. Not with Genevieve's dad now a stronger person of interest. It had to be a coincidence that he'd worked with the first dead girl's dad. Chances were, he'd never even met her. Nick had never met plenty of his colleagues' kids. Well, some of them. A few, at least.

He sighed then went back to his phone and sent Genevieve a text.

Nick: Need to ask your family questions. Here or the condo?

Ending with a question would raise the likelihood of her responding. If not, he'd make a trip over to the condo. He needed to get Walter's side of the story while he was still just a person of interest—before he became a full-blown suspect.

Knock, knock.

Nick glanced over and saw Anderson. He undoubtedly wanted to know if Nick had reached the Fosters yet. Nick waved him in, his mind racing for a good response. Something other than no that wasn't a lie.

Anderson came in. "Are they on their way over?"

Nick drew in a deep breath. "I'm going to head to the condo. That way they don't have to come in again. They've been through enough."

Anderson arched a brow. "Sure you can be unbiased?"

"We all work with Foster," Nick snapped. "Sorry. I just mean that none of us want to see her dad as a suspect. Yes, I can be unbiased. We all want to get to the truth of the matter, nobody more than me. I just want to see the killer put behind bars. That's all any of us want."

"I'm just asking, sir." Anderson nodded and gave him a sympathetic glance. "I can go with you, if you want."

"Find out if forensics has ID'd anyone else. One body doesn't tell us much. The whole group of them will give us a clearer picture."

"You've got it, Captain. Let me know if you change your mind." Anderson studied him for a moment before leaving.

Nick sighed and checked his phone. No new texts.

He gathered his things then headed out to his Mustang, glad to be exiting from the back parking lot. The media circus had grown since the morning.

Nick mulled over all the details he knew about the case as he drove. There weren't usually coincidences in his line of work, but hoped this would be the exception. Genevieve would be crushed if her dad turned out to be the killer. The fact that he lived in the house and had a connection to a victim didn't bode well. That was not one, but two, coincidences.

He reached the condo and parked, his mind racing. Genevieve's car was there. That meant unless she'd gone somewhere with her parents, she was there.

Hopefully she could explain away the coincidences.

It was strange to knock on his condo's door. He'd lived in the tiny unit for what had felt like forever. Time had seemed to stand still during the period when Corrine took the kids across the country from him.

Nick was about to knock again when the door opened.

Genevieve answered, her eyes red and her long dark hair flat. Her eyes widened. "Nick."

"I've been trying to get ahold of you."

"Sorry. It's been crazy around here. Tinsley woke up from a nightmare, and that was after we all slept in pretty late."

He nodded. "Understandable. Mind if I come in?"

She hesitated. "Um, sure. We kind of made a mess. Sorry."

"No problem. I just have a few questions."

Genevieve stepped aside. They went to the kitchen and sat at the table. Tinsley was reclining on the futon, reading. The shower sounded through the thin walls.

Nick cleared his throat. "Is your dad here?"

Her expression darkened for a moment. "He actually went fishing. It's his way of dealing with stress."

Nick managed to keep his face from showing his worry. Walter not only had two coincidences going against him, but now he was out fishing, unable to be questioned? This was looking worse.

It was a good thing he'd convinced Anderson to stay behind. Nick needed to find out what was going on before anyone else caught wind of this.

Genevieve twisted a lock of hair around her finger. "Is everything okay?"

"Actually, it's your dad I wanted to speak with, but maybe you can help."

Her face paled. "Sure. Is there a problem?"

Nick considered his wording, but it really didn't matter how he framed it. She was a cop, and would understand the severity of the situation—that her dad was moving up on the persons-of-interest list.

"Nick?"

"How close was your dad to Gary Michaels?"

She gave him a double-take. "Who?"

"They worked together."

Genevieve tapped the table and looked deep in thought. "I don't recognize the name. Why?"

"Just trying to fill in some gaps."

She frowned. "What kind of gaps? Who is Gary Mitchell?"

"Michaels," Nick corrected. "His daughter went missing some thirty years ago."

Genevieve's face paled even more. "You think my dad...?"

Nick shook his head. "I'm here to clear him of the connection. To get him off the list."

She buried her face in her palms and muttered.

"Can you call him so I can talk to him? I just need to ask him some questions."

"He's not answering our calls." Genevieve looked up at him, her eyes shining with tears. "This looks so bad, but really, fishing is how he deals with stress."

Nick's heart shattered, seeing her pain. He reached for her hand and squeezed. "I'm sure it's all a big misunderstanding. It has to be. That's why I'm here to clear him from the list."

She blinked and tears spilled onto her face. "He always goes to fish when things are tough. He comes back calmer. Happier. It's his way of dealing with things."

He nodded. "I believe you. I just need to be able to talk with him myself. You understand."

"Of course." She wiped her eyes.

"Do you know when he'll be back? Or where he went fishing? I can ask him questions there, where he's comfortable."

"Maybe Mom knows." Genevieve's lips trembled.

Nick couldn't take it a moment longer. He scooted closer, wrapped an arm around her, and brushed his lips across hers. "It's going to be okay. I promise you."

"How can you promise that?"

"Because I'll make sure of it. You have my word."

Genevieve shook in his arms. He got a whiff of a sweet floral aroma. He couldn't take her pain. He needed to do something, so he pressed his mouth onto hers, taking the kiss deeper for just a moment before pulling away. She leaned against his chest and continued shaking.

Nick's heart raced. She could probably hear it thundering in her ears. He tightened his grip around her and rubbed her back.

"Captain Fleshman?"

He turned around to see Brenda, her wet hair in curlers. "Yes, Mrs. Foster. I came to ask a few more questions."

She arched a brow, glancing at Genevieve pressed against his chest.

Nick ignored the look. "I have some questions about your husband that Genevieve couldn't answer. Perhaps you could help?"

"Sure." She sat across from them, still eyeing her daughter who was practically in his lap. "What do you need to know?"

"Do you know a Gary Michaels?"

Brenda's eyes were blank as though she were trying to remember. Then her mouth dropped open. "Don't tell me poor Amy has something to do with this."

"So, your husband did work with Gary?"

She nodded. "Yes. I remember her disappearance like it was yesterday. Was Amy buried under our yard the whole time?" Her eyes grew as wide as saucers.

"I can't speak about the case. I'm sorry."

"I'm going to be sick." She covered her mouth.

Nick cleared his throat. "I should ask Walter the rest of my questions. Do you have an address for where he's fishing?"

Brenda gave a worried glance to Genevieve. "I'm not sure where he went. Sometimes he just takes off when he's stressed—doesn't mean he's guilty."

"Of course not. I'm just here to clear him from any possible connection to the case."

She breathed a sigh of relief. "Well, I can give you the names of the places he often fishes. Would that help?"

"Certainly." Nick pulled out his phone and opened the notes app.

Brenda listed off a few places and Nick jotted them down. "Any others?"

She shook her head. "Do you want his number?"

Nick pulled out his notepad and flipped through, making sure not to disturb Genevieve, who still rested against him. "I've got it here. Is this correct?" He read off the numbers.

Brenda nodded.

"Can I get a few more details? Then I'll be out of your hair."

"Sure."

"What's his full name?"

"Walter Anthony Foster."

Nick scribbled on the paper. "Does he have any nicknames?"

"No..." She looked deep in thought for a moment. "He actually used to go by his middle name when we met."

"Anthony?"

She nodded. "But then later he thought Walter was more distinguished, so he's gone by his given name for over thirty years."

"He doesn't go by that anymore?"

"No. Never." Brenda shook her head.

UNLOAD

Zoey stared into the eyes of her best friend. Her insides shook, and her stomach lurched. Part of her felt relief at the thought of telling her everything. Another part of her wanted to run. Far away.

Pretending none of this was actually happening really wasn't healthy, and she knew it, even if it was easier. Part of her stomach issues were probably due to the stress of keeping everything to herself.

"You know I won't judge you." Macy put her hand on top of Zoey's. "I'm here for you, just like I always have been."

Zoey nodded and took a deep breath. Her heart thundered in her chest faster than it had in a long time. It almost brought her back to her abduction.

She stared at a daisy for a moment before forcing herself to look at Macy. Her hands shook. She shivered despite the warm sun beating down.

"Something else happened, didn't it?" Macy's voice cracked. She squeezed Zoey's hand, heartbreak in her eyes. She knew.

Tears blurred Zoey's vision. There would be no more trying to pretend that the last assault hadn't happened. No more hoping it would all go away. Her best friend had already figured it out. "He... Dave..."

She struggled to find the words. They were there. She just couldn't say them, even though Macy knew. She was just waiting for Zoey to voice it.

Maybe she should just run. Macy had the baby—she wouldn't be able to keep up. No, that would be the cowardly thing to do. And she was no coward. She needed to do this, no matter how hard it was. Macy was her best friend, and she would help her through this. As a counselor, she had resources. Heck, she'd even been abducted herself. That was what had driven her to her profession.

Zoey took another deep breath. "Before I escaped, he raped me."

Tears spilled from Macy's eyes. "Oh, Zoey. I was hoping that wasn't what you were going to say." She wrapped her arms around Zoey as best she could with Caden strapped to her. "Have you told anyone else?"

"The doctors, right after it happened. They collected evidence. I'll have to testify." Zoey swallowed, trying to keep herself together.

"You've been checked out. Good. You haven't talked about it since then?"

Zoey shook her head, and tears spilled onto her face. "Not even to the counselor. I just couldn't do it."

"You didn't get any STD's from him?"

"No, amazingly. Though I think I have to be retested in a few months for one of them. The whole thing is so confusing."

"What does Alex think?"

Zoey didn't respond. She bit her lip.

"He doesn't know?" Macy asked.

"Not yet."

"Are you going to tell him?"

"I'm going to have to soon. Can't hide it forever."

Macy sat back, wide-eyed. "You don't mean…? You're pregnant?"

Zoey pressed her shirt against her stomach, showing off the roundness of her belly. "I'm carrying a psychopath's child."

Macy's mouth gaped. "I had no idea."

"Nobody does."

"Are you planning on keeping it? Are you sure it isn't Alex's? Is that what you're worried about? Maybe it's his. It has to be, right?"

Zoey rubbed her temples. "You're making my head spin."

"Sorry. I can't help freaking out when this involves my best friend and my baby brother."

Zoey groaned. "Great. You're referring to him as your baby brother."

She frowned. "When are you going to tell Alex?"

"Not helping." Zoey closed her eyes and focused on her breathing.

"I'm sorry. What do you need from me? What can I do?"

Zoey opened her eyes. "No more questions, please."

"Understood. I'm sorry. What can I do?"

Zoey pressed her palms on her stomach, but didn't say anything.

Macy frowned. "I'll do anything. Whatever you need, just let me know."

"You already have so much on your plate."

"I also have all the time in the world right now. My maternity leave is six months."

"Thanks." Zoey's voice came out a whisper. She cleared her throat.

"There are ways to check paternity while pregnant, if that's what you're worried about."

Zoey shook her head. "There isn't a question of who the father is, unfortunately."

Macy frowned, her eyes full of pain. "You're a hundred percent sure?"

Zoey just nodded, unable to bring herself to talk more about it. "Have you considered other options? You don't have to keep it."

"This is my *baby*!"

"I know. I'm just saying—"

"Nothing!" Zoey glared at her. "You're saying nothing. I wouldn't terminate Ariana when I got pregnant at fifteen, and I'm not getting rid of this baby, either. I'm also not giving up another child for adoption."

Macy nodded. "Don't you think this is different? Even though you were young, you loved Alex."

Zoey folded her arms. "I still brought a child into this world when people thought I was selfish and stupid for doing so. But look at her now! She's smart and kind and beautiful. I'm well aware of my *options*, but I'm not interested."

"Okay, I just needed to ask. For you."

"Now you know where I stand. If you want to go counselor on me, pick a different topic. Ask how I'm dealing after the rape. What it's doing to me keeping it to myself." Tears blurred her eyes again. "But not this. I know my options, okay? I know them!"

"I'm sorry. I really am."

Zoey turned and looked at the flowers, wiping her eyes as the tears came.

Macy sighed. "If it makes you feel any better, when I told my insurance company that I was pregnant, the first question out of the woman's mouth was if I wanted to have an abortion. I was mortified, and barely kept myself from telling her off. I apologize if I made you feel the way she made me feel that day."

"It's not the same."

"It was still insensitive."

Zoey turned to Macy. "I know you didn't mean any harm. I'm sure it's a natural question, especially given your job. But for me, it's not an option."

Macy nodded. "I just want what's best for you. And for Alex, too. I want to see you guys happy. You're so close to getting everything you deserve."

"That's why this sucks so much."

Macy put her hand on Zoey's arm. "That's not the only reason?"

Zoey shook her head.

Silence rested between them before Macy spoke. "Have you been to a doctor since your examination?"

"Not yet. I…" Zoey's voice trailed off.

"You don't have to explain anything. If you want, I'll go with you."

Gratitude overcame Zoey. She threw her arms around Macy, careful not to disturb Caden. "Thank you."

"What are best friends for?"

"Now I need to tell Alex." Her voice wavered. "Then everyone else."

"One step at a time. Do you want me to set up an appointment for you? Do you still see Dr. Ross?"

"Yes to both. I can't thank you enough."

"It's the least I could do. Then we can figure out when to tell Alex."

Zoey frowned. "He's barely holding on with his busy schedule. I should wait until he's done with the academy."

Macy raised an eyebrow. "You think you can wait that long? That's almost two more months, isn't it?"

Zoey glanced down at her middle. "Well, he isn't likely to notice with as tired as he is."

"In just a few weeks, you won't be able to hide it with loose clothes. From anyone."

Zoey's stomach twisted. "Can we just focus on setting up an appointment for now? I'll make the appointment. Maybe you can hold my hand?"

"You know I will."

ATTEMPT

The school bell would ring in ten minutes for the afternoon recess. And Tony's phone was on silent now.

Nobody was going to get in his way this time.

This recess would be half as long as the one at lunchtime when Gayle had ruined his plans, so he would either have to snatch Maisie or convince her to follow him back to his car—all within just a few minutes.

Or worst case, he would have to build a rapport with her. Build her trust slowly, over time. But today was her birthday. He had a present and a balloon. The helium would be gone this time tomorrow.

Eight minutes.

He checked his phone. As soon as he tapped the button on the side, the picture of Maisie's present and balloon showed. He couldn't bring them to the school grounds, but the picture was almost as good. It would show her what was waiting just for her.

The thought of the little girl sliding her hand into his and strolling back to his car sent a shiver down his back. It was a real possibility. She might come with him in less than a half hour.

He could easily convince her he knows her family. Her mom's

public posts had given him more than enough information—grandparents' names, friends' names, hobbies, family outings, and so much more. All he'd have to do would be to list off a few of those, and the girl would believe everything he said. She'd be putty in his hands.

Then he could bring her to his cabin in the woods. To the special room where he kept his treasures until they joined the others.

His heart sank. Maisie wouldn't be joining any of his other prizes. Even if the cops had left any, they'd be watching the house for a long time.

He couldn't go anywhere near it anytime soon.

Maisie would have to start a new treasure field. She would be alone for a while.

His heart ached at the thought. One thing that eased his mind was that his prizes were able to keep each other company. They were never truly alone.

Now poor Maisie would have to wait all by herself until he got his next treasure. Just like Amy had been alone so long ago. Although she hadn't been alone. Not really. Her family had been there. They just didn't know *she* was there, too.

Maybe he could get a little pet for Maisie so she wouldn't have to be alone until he found his next treasure. Yeah. That was what he would do. He could keep them close to his cabin. Then he could visit them anytime he wanted. Well, within reason. He still had to show up for work on occasion, even though he did most of his work remotely.

He glanced at the time.

Five minutes.

Time to make his way over. He glanced in the mirror and smiled. Perfect. He had it down to an art. The smile that quickly conveyed he was kind and trustworthy. It worked every time.

He double-checked that his phone was on silent. It was, and it didn't show any new missed calls since he'd last checked.

Good. People were finally leaving him alone.

He stuffed the phone in his pocket, practiced his smile again, and headed down the road, staying close to the line of parked cars. The school looked like a ghost town, but it would come to life in a matter of minutes just like it had earlier.

Some cars drove by, then the road was clear. He double-checked traffic and pulled the hood up over his head before crossing the road. Once on the school grounds, he tossed the sweatshirt into a bush to pick up later, and jumped the chain-link fence.

He scoffed. Some security—a lousy fence. Didn't have any cameras pointed toward the area, either. He'd checked and re-checked.

The bell rang. Perfect timing. He walked nonchalantly over to the wall, where he could walk underneath the few cameras pointing toward the doors.

Shrieks and laughter sounded, growing louder and nearer by the moment. His heart raced. The tricky part would be getting off the property unseen with Maisie when she agreed to go with him.

He leaned against the wall like he had every business being there.

Nobody paid him a bit of attention. Kids ran past, heading in all directions. The recess teacher who had been glued to her phone earlier was paying more attention to it than the kids again. The other two teachers would be on the other side of the playground. He could still avoid them if he needed to go around. It was possible.

He scanned the crowd for Maisie, keeping an eye out for long blonde hair and a pink shirt, just like in the photo her mom posted that morning. There weren't actually that many blondes, making it easier.

Then he saw her.

Everything seemed to stand still for a moment. Or maybe five.

Once he regained control of his breathing, his mind raced. She was playing jump rope close to the fence, not far from the distracted teacher.

His heart nearly jumped into his throat and his stomach twisted into knots. Beads of sweat broke out on his forehead.

No matter how many times he'd attempted this—both successfully and unsuccessfully—the thrill never lessened. There was always a risk of being caught. Of the child fighting back. Some did. The risk of something going wrong that he hadn't prepared for, like that one neighborhood dog. He rubbed his hip, just thinking about the mutt who eventually paid for that. Buried like one of his treasures, but nowhere near them.

Maisie stormed away from the kid playing rope.

Right toward him.

His skin prickled with excitement, and his breath hitched. He glanced around, looking for the other teachers.

Still out of sight.

Little Maisie stomped right by him.

He let her get a few feet away before speaking. "Maisie."

She spun around. Confusion covered her face as she studied him.

"Are you okay?" He took one step closer, widening his eyes to give the appearance of innocence. Like a sad puppy.

Maisie pursed her lips. "Who are you?"

"I'm the new janitor, remember? Tony."

She scratched her head. But she didn't step away.

He took another step closer. "Why do you look sad, Maisie? You shouldn't be sad on your birthday."

"You know it's my birthday?"

"How could I forget a day as special as that?"

Maisie's stance relaxed. She tilted her head.

"I actually found something you would like. When I saw it at the store, I knew you'd love it."

She hesitated.

He lowered himself closer to her level. "Everyone deserves to have a happy birthday. What did those kids do to upset you?"

Maisie frowned, and her mouth trembled. "Those kids are always mean to me."

"To you? Who would do that?" He glanced over at the kids playing jump rope. "Let me guess. It's that bossy girl with the short blue skirt causing the problems. Am I right?"

She nodded and sighed. "Yeah. Mommy says Camry's jealous."

"I bet she is." He gave her the most sympathetic look he could muster. "You're so much prettier."

"I am?" Maisie glanced over at the little brat.

"Much. Hey, do you want to see a picture of the present?"

She played with a lock of her hair and smiled shyly. "Okay."

He pulled out his phone and showed her the picture of the balloon and wrapped present in his car.

Maisie's eyes lit up. "Those are for me?"

"Yeah. If you want them."

"Mommy said I'm not supposed to take things from strangers."

"I'm not a stranger." He smiled brightly. "Tony the janitor, remember?"

"Oh, yeah."

"Do you want to come and see? They're yours. We just have to get them out of my car."

She brought a finger to her mouth. "I don't know…"

He glanced up at the recess teacher. She was no longer staring at her screen.

The woman was staring right at him.

He turned back to Maisie. "Speaking of jealous people, that recess teacher is headed my way. She hates me. Don't tell her anything I told you, okay?"

"Um…" Maisie looked to the side.

"If you say anything, I can't give you the present. If you stay quiet, I'll give that to you later."

He ran.

QUESTION

Nick pulled into the parking lot, which was nothing more than a patch of grass cleared out between the road and the water. Only two other vehicles were parked there, but one matched the description of Walter's car.

He checked the plates.

Walter's car. Of course, this was the last place on Nick's list to check.

After checking two other fishing sites, and driving over a hundred and fifty miles altogether, his body ached from the stress of traffic and searching for Genevieve's father.

He called in his location and asked for an update on the case.

"They're done digging up around the house. A few officers are still going through the house and shed for clues, but now the priority is identifying the victims and finding the killer."

"Thanks, Tracey. I'll let you know what I find here." Nick ended the call and twisted his neck until he felt a relieving pop. Then he turned it the other way with the same result before downing the rest of his now-cold coffee and heading outside.

The fresh air was nice. He took in a deep breath of pine and saltwater as he stretched. Then he headed for the water. The bubbling waves and quacking ducks relaxed him.

He wouldn't mind sitting down and doing some fishing himself.

It only took a minute to reach the water, but nobody was in sight. Nick looked up and down the rocky shore. Faded footprints went in both directions, so it was a toss-up which direction to go.

He went right, because why not? Rocks of all sizes covered the shore, making his trek a bit of a challenge, but Nick found that he enjoyed it. The fresh air filled his lungs and gave him renewed energy.

After about fifteen minutes, he was ready to turn around when the trees cleared, showing a snow-capped mountain in the distance right in between them.

He stared in awe for a moment, then snapped a picture with his phone and made a mental note to bring the kids here. It was places like this that made the nine months of cold rain worth living in the Pacific Northwest. It really was the best place in the world.

Nick glanced into the trees, trying to see if anyone was in sight. But it was just him and nature.

A bit reluctant, he spun around and marched the other way, eventually passing the area he had first come to, and he kept going. If he didn't find Walter, they might have to consider that he fled. Then he would definitely move from a person of interest to a suspect.

He hated to do that to Genevieve, but her dad sure wasn't making anything easy. It was looking more and more like he had something to hide.

Nick kept going down the shore for another fifteen or twenty minutes. The sun was starting to get lower. His stomach rumbled.

He was about to turn around when he saw something.

Someone fishing.

That someone looked an awful lot like Walter.

Nick picked up his pace, stumbling over the stones.

The man didn't look his way until Nick was almost there.

It was Walter. He wore a dirty gray hoodie and his hair was messy. Almost as though it was wind-blown, but there was hardly a breeze.

"Captain Fleshman?" Walter reeled in the line and set the pole down.

Nick nodded. "Walter. Been looking for you. Haven't been answering your calls when there's an investigation at your house?"

He rose and pulled out his phone. "It's on airplane mode again. How'd that happen?" Walter swiped his finger around the screen. "I keep saying I'm too old for a smartphone. Or maybe not smart enough." He held it up. "Fixed. Did you find anything?"

"Have a seat." Nick gestured toward the log Walter had been sitting on before, and they both sat.

Walter raked his fingers through his hair. "Everything okay?"

"There are bodies in your backyard."

"I mean, aside from that."

Nick cleared his throat. "Where've you been all day?"

"Fishing, mostly." Walter glanced out at the water. "Not much is biting, though. Looks like I'm going home empty-handed."

They sat in silence. Nick waited for Walter to continue.

"Do you want to join me? I've got an extra pole."

"Sure." If they were distracted with fishing, Walter would probably be more likely to say more than he otherwise would.

It only took a few minutes, then they both had lines in the water.

"You come here often?" Nick asked.

Walter sighed. "Yeah, when I'm stressed. But usually, I get fish. Maybe they're just enjoying the sun today."

"Maybe. You been here all day?"

"Mostly. Been moving up and down the shore. Not that it's done me much good."

"What do you think of the bodies being found in your yard?"

Walter turned to him, his expression perplexed. "What do I *think* of it?"

Nick nodded.

"It's horrible. Who would do such a thing?"

"Are you shocked?"

"Of course. My family and I have been out there working on that garden. I never would have expected that."

Nick nodded again. When Walter didn't continue, he spoke. "Did you know anyone else who lived there?"

"What? No."

"Not even Gary Michaels?"

Walter turned to him, his face paling. "What did you say?"

"Gary Michaels." Nick enunciated each syllable.

"He... he lived there? In our house?" Walter's eyes widened.

"When his daughter went missing, actually."

Walter's face paled even more. "They...? He...? I think I'm going to be sick."

"So, you didn't know about any of that?"

"No. I barely knew the man. I was just an intern, and he was in management. Our paths rarely crossed."

"You never knew his daughter? Amy?"

Walter's brows came together. "What are you getting at? Do I need a lawyer?"

Nick shook his head. "I'm just trying to clear you from being a person of interest. You can ask Genevieve. That's how we handle these things. Unfortunately, you have some coincidences linking you to the case. I want to get you off the list so we can find the guy who actually did this. Do you think Gary was capable of it?"

"Is he a suspect?"

"I'm not at liberty to discuss that."

Walter frowned. "Like I said, I never really knew the guy. I wasn't there long. It was just an internship for college."

"How long were you there?"

"A year. Well, nine months—a school year."

Nick nodded, keeping his expression vague. "What did other people say about him?"

Walter swallowed. "I don't know. It was a long time ago."

"You said he was in management. I know those types. Did he like to lord it over people? He probably stepped on some toes to get where he was. That's how it works."

"Well, I suppose. Come to think of it, there were some guys in the mailroom who couldn't stand him. Said he was a real jerk. I don't remember any details."

Nick studied Genevieve's dad. If what he said was true, he would quickly be removed from their list.

"What are you thinking? I get the feeling I need a lawyer."

"No. We're done for now. In the meantime, stick closer to home and keep your phone off airplane mode in case we need to ask you any more questions. That's the best thing you can do for yourself at this point."

"Sure thing. Sorry about that."

"It could happen to anyone." Nick rose, then something tugged on his line. He turned to Walter. "I thought the fish weren't biting today."

"You're a luckier fisherman than me, Captain."

EXHAUSTED

Alex pulled up to the curb in front of his future in-laws' home and took a deep breath. Physical Training had been rough—twice as long and three times as challenging.

He'd been tempted to stay at the academy to sleep, but he couldn't because it was Friday. Also, he'd promised Ariana another visit. She was used to him being there every day after school, but that wasn't possible with the rigorous schedule as a cadet living over fifty miles away.

Tap, tap!

Alex glanced over at the passenger side window.

Ari stood there, waving and smiling.

A little energy ran through him. Not much, but enough to pull him out of the car.

"You made it!" Ariana ran around and threw her arms around him.

He embraced her and kissed the top of her head. "You sound surprised."

Ari shrugged. "Mimi said you might be tired."

"I told you I'd be here, and I meant it."

She stepped back. "Come see what I've added to my science project!"

"Let's see it." Alex shut his door and remote-locked the car. He followed her as she bounced up the driveway.

At the door, she turned around. "Oh, and Scout's here. Seems like he wants to see you."

"How's he doing?" Alex wasn't sure how much his daughter knew, but her boyfriend had recently witnessed some murders and Alex had been there right after to comfort the boy. Since then, the two had developed a strong, but mostly unspoken, bond.

"He's good." Ariana smiled. "He's helping me paint the box part of my project."

Alex waved to Kenji and Valerie, who were watching a baseball game on the TV. They both waved back, then Kenji shouted at the screen. He'd been a professional baseball player in Japan and took the game seriously.

At the kitchen table, Scout was hunched over a box, painting it neon green.

"My dad's here," Ariana announced. "I'm going to run up to my room and grab those charts I was telling you about. I think I need to fix that one part." She spun around and disappeared before her boyfriend could respond.

Scout set the brush down and glanced up at Alex. "Hi, Mr. Mercer."

"You make me feel ancient. I'm serious when I say to call me Alex."

"My parents said that's rude. You're an adult."

Alex leaned closer. "Maybe *they're* ancient."

Scout chuckled.

"But don't tell them I said that."

"I won't."

"Then call me Alex. You can call me Mr. Mercer in front of them. Deal?" Alex held out his hand.

Scout smiled and shook. "Deal."

Alex shook his hand out. "Ouch. You've got quite the grip."

Scout shook his head and laughed.

They both grabbed a brush and painted the box without speaking for a minute.

"How are you doing?" Alex kept his gaze on the box.

Scout sighed. "I'm still having nightmares. I see the blood spray on the window over and over. It doesn't stop."

"You're still seeing a therapist?"

"Yeah. Not that it's helping much. He wants to medicate me, but my parents don't want that."

Alex glanced at him. "What do you want?"

Scout shrugged. "Mom says the medications make people sleep a lot, and they could mess up my brain chemistry. What do you think?"

"I don't know anything about that. I've heard both good things and bad things about side effects of antidepressants. They might help you be able to deal with what you saw, then you could stop taking them later. But like I said, I don't really know. My sister could probably tell you more. She's a counselor, and I think she took some antidepressants for a while."

"That might help. I don't want them to change me. My cousin was on some for a while, and they ruined her eyesight. Now she has to wear glasses for the rest of her life. That sucks. She never even knew that was something that could happen. The doctor didn't tell her it was a rare side effect until after."

Alex set his brush down. "Sounds like you might have your answer."

"I guess." Scout took a deep breath. "I hate the nightmares, though."

"How are you getting by during the day?"

"Tired but okay. It helps that we're not at the same school building. I don't have to pass that spot where it happened." He shuddered.

"That sounds good. Have you tried journaling?"

Scout shook his head.

"Try it. That helped me when my sister was kidnapped. You can get all your anger and worries out without having to tell anyone how you actually feel. It's all a secret."

He looked like he was considering it.

Ding-dong!

"Scout, your dad's here!" Kenji called.

Ariana bounced down the stairs with an armful of papers. She dumped them on the table, then took Scout's hand and walked with him to the door.

Alex watched the two, his heart warming. It reminded him of when he and Zoey had first admitted their feelings for each other.

With any luck, Scout and Ari wouldn't make the same mistakes he and Zoey had made. Not just getting pregnant, but also smoking, drinking, and sneaking out. He didn't want to see Ariana go down that path.

Alex shuddered. He felt bad for what he'd put his parents through. But they hadn't known the half of it. The pregnancy had been a total shock. But that was when Macy was missing, so they were beyond distracted.

Scout kissed the back of Ariana's hand, then disappeared out the door. She waved and closed it before returning to the kitchen.

"What do you think of the green? Is it too bright?"

"It's eye-catching. I think it's perfect."

"Oh, good!" She clapped. "Hey, Grandma and Grandpa called. They made pie and have ice cream. Wanna go over there?" Ari pleaded with her eyes, making it impossible for him to say no.

"Sure. Let's go. Do they know I'm here?"

She threw her arms around him. "Yeah. They saw your car out front."

That explained the call. He hadn't seen his parents in over a week, despite coming next door to see Ariana so often. "Let's clear the table first."

Ari pouted. "But there's pie next door. Grandma's special cherry pie."

Alex's mouth watered at the thought. "You don't think Mimi will mind the messy table?"

"Just go!" Valerie called from the other room.

"See?" Ari threw him a playful glance.

Alex's phone beeped with a text. "Must be Grandma." He glanced down to check.

It wasn't his mom. The text was from an unknown number.

Unknown: Flynn wants to see you.

TEXTS

Alex stared at his phone's screen, trying not to reveal his shock and other raging emotions from the mysterious and ominous text.

"Come on, Dad." Ari pulled on his arm. "The dessert."

He shoved the phone in his pocket and forced a smile. "Wouldn't want to miss that."

She dragged him down the hallway and to the door.

"Are you going somewhere?" Kenji asked as they passed the living room.

"Grandma made pie!" Ariana opened the door. "And for some reason Dad doesn't seem interested."

"He looks exhausted," Kenji said. "You can sleep here if you need to, Alex. I know you have your old room next door, but you're always welcome here."

"Thanks. I appreciate it." Alex threw him an appreciative glance before Ari yanked him outside.

As they crossed the yards, the sweet aroma of the pie drifted their way.

"Do you smell that?" Ariana tugged him toward his parents' house.

"I think the whole neighborhood can." His mouth watered, but as delicious as it smelled, it wasn't enough to make him forget the text.

Flynn wanted to see him? In jail or somewhere else? The man was somehow able to walk around free while at the same time being in prison across the state.

Ariana pulled him to the front door and swung it open. "We're here!"

Alex's mom poked her head over the railing at the top of the stairs and smiled. "Perfect timing! Ice cream with your slices?"

"Of course." Ariana grinned. "Let me help."

She ran up the stairs while Alex trudged up, his legs feeling like lead weights. His old bedroom actually sounded pretty good.

By the time he reached the kitchen, Ariana was already scooping vanilla ice cream onto the plates.

Mom wrapped her arms around him. "How are you doing? It looks like they've been running you ragged."

"It's no boot camp, but yeah. I can't tell you how glad I am it's the weekend. I could sleep for both days."

Ari turned around, her eyes filled with disappointment. "You're going to sleep all weekend?"

He shook his head. "No, but I could. Easily." He yawned, as if to prove his point.

Mom smiled. "Your room is always here if you need it. Sleep here tonight, then go home tomorrow if you want. We always love the company."

"I may just take you up on that."

Both she and Ariana grinned.

Alex helped them set up the table, then his dad came in. "It's our favorite cadet!"

"Do you know any others?"

"No, but you're still our favorite. It's great to see you." He gave Alex a bear hug.

They made small talk over pie and ice cream. The adults drank coffee, and Ariana had hot cocoa.

Alex tried to push the text out of his mind, but he couldn't stop thinking about it. Running into Flynn the night before had to have been on purpose. It couldn't have been an accident.

Not with the text.

"Alex?" His mom's voice brought him back to the kitchen.

He shook his head. "Sorry. I'm tired."

"You look like you have a lot on your mind." She gave him a sympathetic smile. "Anything we can do?"

"No. This is great. Dessert with family. What more could I ask for?"

"Maybe for academy to be over," Ariana chimed in.

"Definitely that. I hate being so far away from everyone."

"How far is it, exactly?" Dad asked.

Alex yawned again. "Over fifty miles. That's how I qualified for the dorms. If it was much farther away, I wouldn't even be able to think about coming home a couple times a week, like I've been managing so far."

Ari wrapped her arms around him. "I'm so glad you do."

Mom brought the pie over to the table. "Seconds, anyone?"

"Me!" Ari scooped the last bite on her plate into her mouth.

Alex chuckled and took another piece also, finding his exhaustion and annoyance melting away. He wasn't sure if it was from being with his family or from the caffeine, but he was grateful for the reprieve.

Once they were all too full for any more pie, his mom talked them into playing cards. They laughed and teased each other while playing several different games until it was dark outside.

"Can I spend the night, too?" Ari begged.

Alex's mom kissed the top of her head. "I'd love that, but you'll need to ask Mimi and Papi."

A half hour later, Alex kissed Ari goodnight in Macy's old room. Then he lumbered into his childhood bedroom, the effects of the coffee now gone. Hopefully, Ariana and his parents would let him sleep in. He needed it after such a long and tiring week.

The mattress welcomed him like an old friend. He pulled up the familiar covers and breathed in their fresh scent.

Just as he was drifting off, his phone beeped with another text. He checked it in case it was Zoey, but it wasn't.

It was from the same number as earlier. And the message was exactly the same as the other one.

Unknown: Flynn wants to see you.

Anger churned in his gut.

Alex: Who is this?

Unknown: Flynn wants to see you.

Alex: Who. Is. This!!!

Unknown: Flynn wants to see you.

Alex: I'm about 2 block u.

Unknown: U don't want 2 do that.

At least it was a different text. Alex waited, wanting to make the person at the other end sweat, thinking he had blocked him.

Unknown: Flynn wants to see you.

Alex: Where?

Unknown: The prison of course.

Alex was pretty sure victims couldn't visit criminals in prison, but his mind was also swimming in criminal law. Also, technically *he* wasn't the victim. His daughter had been.

Unknown: Hello?

Alex: Leave me alone.

Unknown: You gonna visit Flynn?

Alex: I'll think about it.

Unknown: Flynn wants to see you.

Alex resisted the urge to throw his phone against the wall.

Alex: I'm busy these days.

Unknown: Is the academy fun?

Alex: Who is this??

Acid churned in his gut. It infuriated him that the person knew he was in the academy. Were they watching him? Did they have access to those records?

Alex waited a full five minutes for another text, which didn't come. He silenced his phone and settled back down under the blankets, making a mental note to find out if he could actually visit Flynn in the prison.

Maybe he'd be able to find out what was going on once and for all. There were people who thought he was nuts for his claims of seeing Flynn out free. But he knew what he'd seen. He could never forget the face of the man who had abducted his daughter.

And the man he'd seen last night and on a few other occasions was Flynn Myer—no matter what anyone else said.

WORRY

Genevieve tucked in Tinsley's blankets then left the room, closing the door behind her. In the living room, she exchanged a concerned glance with her mom.

Dad still wasn't home, and it was dark now. He'd been gone all day.

Nick had let her know he'd found him fishing but didn't go into any detail other than saying he was safe and still not a suspect as there was no evidence linking him to anything.

That should've helped her to feel better, but it didn't. If enough coincidences pointed to her dad, he could become a suspect. And he sure wasn't helping matters by disappearing all day and not answering anyone's calls.

"Tinsley asleep?" Mom asked.

Genevieve nodded. "She seems to be in better spirits since all of this happened. She's actually been talking, and she even gave Nick—I mean the captain—a hug."

"Is something going on between you and the captain?"

Genevieve's face flamed. Luckily, the room was dim and her mom couldn't see her blush. "What makes you ask that?"

"You just called him by his first name, for one thing. Then there's the fact that you were in his arms earlier."

"He was offering me comfort. We're friends. His kids are friends with Tinsley. Is there something wrong with that?"

"Isn't he your boss?"

"Doesn't mean we can't be friends."

Mom gave her a knowing look.

"Have you heard from dad yet?"

"He'll be back. And don't change the subject. Is the captain the reason you're taking a break from work?"

"I'm going to get some air." She marched toward the door.

"Genevieve, I'm not judging you. I just don't want to see you putting your career on the line. You've wanted to be a police officer since you were a girl. Everything you've done has been for this."

"You think I don't know that? I'm not going to do anything stupid." Not again, anyway. "If Tinsley wakes, tell her I'll be back soon, would you?"

Mom frowned, but then nodded. "Are you just going to be outside, or are you going somewhere?"

"I'm not sure yet." She stepped outside and took a deep breath. As if it weren't bad enough that she was falling more in love with her boss every day, now her mom knew. Or at the very least, suspected.

She couldn't return to work and have a relationship with her captain, nor could she go back and see him every day at work and not have a relationship with him. It was hard to think around him. Her mind turned to mush and she went weak in the knees.

Genevieve hadn't been able to stop thinking about being in his arms earlier. His strong, muscular arms. Pressed against his firm chest. His dusting of a beard scratching against her cheek.

Maybe what she needed wasn't air, but rather a cold shower. Ice cold.

Brakes squealed as a car pulled into the parking lot.

She squinted to see. Her heart skipped a beat when she recognized the car. Dad was finally home.

Genevieve leaned against the door and waited as he pulled into a spot, then took his time getting out. Even in the dim light, she could tell he was exhausted as he plodded toward her.

When he stopped a few feet away, the porch light revealed even more. Dark bands rested underneath his eyes, his skin was pale, and his hair was messy, like he'd been pulling at it.

"You okay?" She didn't budge from the door.

He nodded. "I need to get inside. Long day."

"Where have you been?"

"Fishing."

"All day?"

He sighed and grimaced, the lines on his face all looking more pronounced. "Mostly."

"Mostly? What else did you do?"

"We can talk about it later. Let me in."

She shook her head. "This isn't a joke, Dad. You're moving up on the persons of interest list, and you're acting as guilty as sin."

"A man can't go to the water to think? To get away from everything?"

"Sure, but with everything going on, it looks bad. Especially since you're not answering anyone's calls."

"I talked to that police captain. I told him my phone was accidentally on airplane mode. He was fine with it. Let me in, so I can get to bed."

"Did you really know one of the victim's dads?"

He threw his head back. "Barely. We worked in the same place. I already explained all of this to him. Step aside before I move you myself."

"I beg your pardon?"

"I'm too tired to deal with this. You're my daughter. I don't need this from you."

She gritted her teeth. "I'm also an adult, and I'm involved with this mess, too. We all are."

"We can talk in the morning, Genevieve. For now, I need a shower and a long sleep."

"Fine. I'd recommend not taking off." She stepped aside.

"And I'm going to keep my phone off airplane mode, too." He flung open the door, marched inside, and slammed it shut.

Genevieve flinched at the noise, then glared at the door as if he could see her through it.

What was going on with him? Was he really that clueless? Or did he just not care how his actions looked to everyone else? Nick was trying to clear his name, but Dad wasn't doing a thing to help himself.

Hopefully the facts would be enough to clear him, because he was doing everything to shove himself onto the suspect list.

Genevieve stormed inside and went straight to bed. She needed to focus on herself and Tinsley for the time being. That and finding another precinct to work for, because she wanted to see what could happen between her and Nick more than she wanted her current job.

PARTY

Tony lowered his baseball cap as more shrieking kids ran past. One girl wore a shirt that read, *Birthday Girl*. It wasn't Maisie. She and her mom were still setting up their party room.

Maisie's mom was practically asking for him to come and take her. She'd posted all the details of Maisie's party publicly. It was like she wanted someone to come and snatch the girl. Why else would she post such details for the world to see?

Another group of kids raced by. All boys this time, somehow managing to wrestle as they ran. One kid punched another in the eye, then both laughed.

Girls weren't like that. They were much more dignified. When they fought, they didn't leave any marks. Their weapons were words, and once they got older, they knew how to use them to wound far deeper than any physical injury.

All of them. Every single one. None made it out of the teenage years without that magical deathly ability.

As if to prove his point, his phone rang.

It was Gayle.

Again.

Why had he decided having a girlfriend would be a good idea?

No good ever came from it. What he needed was to get women out of his life—all of them. They were bossy, vindictive things. Far more trouble than they were worth.

Maisie raced by, giggling with one of the girls she'd been upset with at the jump rope the day before. How could she have invited that little brat who had upset her so much?

He had half a mind to tell that girl off and scare her so bad, she'd never pick on another soul for the rest of her life. That would do the world a service. But this was neither the time nor the place. Besides, he couldn't risk a scene.

If he was going to lure Maisie out to his car, where he had a fresh balloon to go with the present, he would need to keep a low profile. He needed to look like he belonged there, and putting a brat in her place wasn't the way to accomplish that.

Patience was what he needed. And lots of it. That was how he had managed to earn all of his previous treasures. The girls who were sweet and never talked back. Well, eventually, they all did. They were part of the female species, after all. That was why they had to be buried.

Maybe Maisie would be different. He always held out hope that his current prize would be the one. There had to be *one* out there he could groom to stay sweet and lovely. That was all he needed. Just one.

Maisie definitely had the potential. Her idiot parents didn't deserve her. That much was clear.

He turned in his chair and watched as she bounced on one trampoline after another, laughing with other kids. Three girls and two boys chased after each other, jumping from one springboard to the next, darting around other groups of kids.

The loudspeaker squeaked, giving him the shivers. A high-pitched voice called for a boy's birthday party.

Maisie and her friends exited the section of trampolines they were playing at and bounded toward a foam pit.

He kept his distance, watching them from the corner of his eye so it wasn't obvious he was following them.

A couple of Maisie's friends left the foam pit and headed toward him. He stuck his hand out for a high-five, and both kids gave him one as they passed. Another group raced by, all giving him fist-bumps.

Before long, each kid who passed him either gave him a high-five or a fist-bump. A few minutes later, Maisie's other two friends exited the foam pit, but she remained.

His pulse pounded throughout his body and his skin tingled. Once she came his way, he'd be able to talk to her alone. Build more rapport. Maybe even convince her to come to the car for his present—though that would be a tough sell with a pile sitting on a table in her party room.

Maisie's parents walked right by him—he recognized them as quickly as he did Maisie, thanks to all of her mom's selfies. She loved the camera, that one. No surprise she took what had to be a hundred pictures of the birthday girl before she joined a friend and snapped pictures of kids on the trampolines. The dad stayed, clapping and calling out to Maisie.

Today would most likely be a day to earn her trust a little more. He was nothing if not patient. He'd follow them home and see if she was the type of kid who was allowed to play outside without adult supervision.

The helicopter parents rarely allowed it these days, but there were still plenty of lazy parents who just didn't care. He still wasn't sure which kind Maisie's parents were. The mom was most likely a helicopter, but the dad could be the opposite. When the parents were a mixture, the kid always ended up outside unattended at some point.

That was one of the situations where patience paid off. He only needed one lax parent. That was all it took. And if the dad was lax, Maisie's parents were the perfect set for him—the mom would feed him everything he needed to know about the girl and the dad would allow her to walk right into the car.

All he needed was a little time. It was all he ever really needed. Only rarely did patience not pay off.

His palms grew moist and waves of excitement ran through him. The buildup was always just as exciting as the taking and the treasuring.

Maisie continued playing in the foam pit until her name was called over the loudspeakers.

Her dad called to her. She groaned loudly before climbing out and marching his way. Her dad pointed in the direction of the party room, walked ahead of her, and spoke to someone who worked there.

Maisie glanced over at him, then spun around and jumped back into the foam pit. She climbed out pretty quickly and raced toward her parents.

She skidded to a stop and gave him a funny expression. Her brows knit together. "You're the school janitor. Why are you here?"

He stepped close and leaned next to her. "Call me Tony, remember. I still have that balloon and present any time you're ready."

Her angelic face lit up. "I'm getting a whole bunch of presents upstairs!"

He nodded. "Like I said, whenever you're ready. Better get to your party!"

She scampered up the stairs.

Patience. That was what would pay off.

DISCUSSION

"Come on, Ava!" Nick leaned against the door and craned his neck inside the house to see his oldest daughter.

"I'm almost ready," she called from down the hall. Probably in the bathroom. She spent more time in there than in her bedroom these days.

Parker and Hanna ran around the front yard, chasing each other. Hanna squealed every time her older brother got too close.

Nick poked his head back inside. "We're leaving! Genevieve and Tinsley are already at the park."

"Hold on, Dad! You're so impatient."

Nick held back a smile. He should probably be annoyed with his teenage daughter, but he was too happy to have his kids back again. They were with him full-time now, and Ava was safe and sound after being held captive by her mother's ex-boyfriend.

Now Corrine had a jail sentence. She wouldn't get out before any of the kids were done with school. While he hated that his kids had to grow up with their mom behind bars, it did make *his* life a lot easier.

Hanna and Parker came over to Nick, huffing and puffing from their game of chase.

"Are we going yet?" Hanna asked between breaths.

He gestured inside. "That's up to your sister."

"Ava!" Hanna shouted.

Nick covered his ears. "Not so loud."

Hanna marched past him and down the hall. "Come on, Ava! You look fine. I wanna see Tinsley."

A minute later, his youngest pulled his oldest out the door. "Lock it, Daddy!"

Nick chuckled, then closed and locked the front door. He turned around and noticed how much makeup Ava had on. He almost said something, but stopped himself.

After being abducted, she hadn't worn any for a while. Or spent time with friends, unless Nick invited them over for her. Though he'd prefer her to wear less eyeliner and lighter-colored lipstick, at least she was getting back into her old routines. He sure wasn't going to complain about her being a normal teenager.

They made their way to his Mustang, and the kids chatted over each other the whole way to the park. Nick interjected his thoughts every so often but mostly just enjoyed listening to them.

With everything going on at work, he'd only had time to get them ready for bed the last couple nights. They'd spent more time with his parents than him. But now that things were slowing down at work—everyone was waiting on the bodies to be identified—he could enjoy his weekend, not only with the kids but also with Genevieve. If he had his way, they'd get the kids together the following day, too.

"There they are!" Hanna rolled down the window and waved at Tinsley as Nick drove around the lot, looking for a spot.

As soon as he set the parking break, the kids piled out and raced each other. If only he could bottle that energy and use some of it himself.

By the time he made it over to the field, the kids had already dispersed, having found others to play with. Even Ava was chatting with Braylon, one of their neighbors. She had to have told him they'd be there, as they were halfway across town. Tinsley and Hanna were looking at flowers, and Parker had joined a game of tackle Frisbee.

Genevieve waved at him and smiled.

Nick's insides turned to mush. If they weren't in the middle of a park, he'd pull her close and kiss her until he couldn't see straight. Instead, he gave her a friendly hug. "How are you holding up?"

She glanced over at Tinsley then back at Nick. "Better. We all got some more sleep last night."

"I'm glad to hear it. Do you need anything else?"

"No. You've already done more than enough."

"Well, I'm happy to do more." His gaze lingered on hers and took in her beauty—her long black hair, enchanting gray eyes, perfectly tanned skin, and full lips. Which were moving. She was speaking, and Nick didn't know what about. He stepped back and focused.

She was talking about Tinsley doing better since the day they'd found the bones. "Is it weird that it's seemed to help her?"

He thought about Tinsley's life before coming to Genevieve—her dad had been killed robbing a bank, and the girl had been forced to help her mom abduct and torture grown men. "Maybe it's a sense of familiarity. Or it could've reminded her of what things used to be like, and now she realizes how good she has it. It's hard to say. Has she seen her therapist?"

Genevieve shook her head. "Not since then. She has an appointment on Monday."

"I'd bring that up, but I wouldn't worry too much about it. Progress is progress."

She glanced back over at Tinsley, who was now swinging with Hanna. Both girls were laughing.

Nick wasn't sure he'd ever seen Tinsley laugh.

"Want to sit?" Genevieve nodded toward a nearby bench.

They sat, and she slid her soft hand into his. He threaded his fingers through hers and scooted closer, not leaving any space between them.

"I'm worried about my dad." She sighed. "He went fishing again this morning. Left a note, at least. My mom called, but he didn't answer. He did text her back, but they didn't actually speak."

"That's how he deals with stress normally? Goes fishing?"

"Or hunting. Or whatever the weather allows. Mom says he's just one of those guys who can't sit still. She tries to keep him busy with their garden, but he still wants to get out in nature by himself. I can't get it through his head that right now it makes him look guilty. He's not," she added quickly.

Nick squeezed her hand. "There are plenty of guys like him. They throw themselves into work or a hobby, no matter how it affects those around them. Or how it might look in times like this."

She met his gaze. "Do you do that?"

"I don't think so, but Corrine's biggest complaint was that I spent too much time at work. You know how it is as an officer, especially when there's a big case. We seem to get so many of them around here. More than towns far bigger than ours."

Genevieve nodded. "Yeah, my last relationship ended for similar reasons."

Which meant they would understand each other if they ever had a relationship. That thought hung in the air between them, unspoken.

Nick traced her palm with his thumb, and they sat in a comfortable silence, watching the kids play. Parker took a pretty good hit, but gave back twice as hard to the kid. Hanna and Tinsley were now spinning on a tire swing. Ava and Braylon were playing a competitive match of tetherball.

Nick's phone alerted him of a text. It was tempting to ignore it, but with such a high-profile case at work, he couldn't ignore anything.

He pulled out his phone and glanced at the text, his stomach twisting.

"What is it?" Genevieve's eyes widened.

Nick met her gaze. "They've identified the twins you found."

TRUTH

Zoey unlocked the door and walked into her parents' house. Everything was quiet.

"Hello?"

Nothing.

Zoey glanced at her fitness watch for the time. She was only a couple minutes early. "Ari!"

Silence.

Maybe they'd gone out for breakfast and had decided to go shopping or for a walk to enjoy the outdoors. She wandered into the kitchen for something to drink, and as she was pouring herself a glass of juice, she noticed her parents out back.

She took the drink with her and went to the backyard. "Is Ari out here?"

Her mom glanced up from the bush she was trimming and wiped her forehead. "No, she spent the night next door. Alyssa made pie last night, then a big pancake breakfast this morning. She managed to get both Ari and Alex to stay the night."

Alex was there, too? Zoey's stomach knotted. She'd really been hoping to avoid him and the whole conversation they needed to have. "Thanks, Mom." She forced a smile. "I'm supposed to take

Ari to play with Tinsley at the park. Do you need her back at a specific time?"

"No, but she needs to be back in time to work on her science project for a few hours."

"Oh, that's right. I'll make sure she's back in plenty of time."

She said goodbye to her parents, then headed over to Chad and Alyssa's house. With any luck, Alex would still be sleeping. It was already nearing one-thirty, though. Even with how much he'd been sleeping on the weekends lately, it was doubtful. Especially with Ariana there.

Zoey knocked. A minute later, Chad answered. "Oh, hey Zoey. You know you can just come in."

"Thanks. Mom said Ari's here?"

He nodded. "Alyssa's showing her how to make stew in the slow cooker."

"Oh, fun."

Chad moved aside and let her in. Zoey headed up the stairs. When she reached the top, she nearly crashed into Alex.

So much for him being asleep. She forced another smile—something she'd been doing a lot of lately—and hugged him, careful to keep her stomach from pressing against him.

He smiled widely. "What a nice surprise. What brings you here?"

"I'm taking Ari to play with Tinsley."

Alex traced her cheek with his fingertip and gazed into her eyes. "Any chance you have a few minutes before you need to leave?"

Zoey glanced away. "Not really. Sorry." She wasn't, though. It was a relief to put off the inevitable conversation. Maybe she could manage to wait until the following weekend. Or better yet, until he was done with the academy. But Macy was right. She'd be showing before then.

He brushed his lips across hers. "Maybe I could go with you?"

Her heart fluttered. She hated to say no to him. "Genevieve and I were going to talk. You know, woman to woman."

"Oh." Disappointment washed over his face. "What about dinner? I could take you out somewhere. Your choice. Just the two of us, or with Ari."

Guilt stung. He just wanted to spend time with her. And if it weren't for her secret, she would want the same.

She swallowed. "That sounds really nice. I'll check with my parents and see if they have plans for her tonight."

He kissed her, deepening the kiss for a moment. "I'll head home and get some rest first. I didn't sleep in as long as I'd hoped."

"Sorry, Dad!" Ari's voice had a song to it as she bounced over. She threw her arms around Zoey. "Are we going to the park now, Mom?"

"Yep. Genevieve says Tinsley can't wait to see you."

Zoey's phone played a jingle in her purse. She pulled it out to see a text.

Genevieve: I'm sorry. Tinsley's really tired. Reschedule?

Zoey's heart sank. She'd really been looking forward to the playdate. Or had she been more excited about avoiding her inevitable talk with Alex?

Zoey: No problem. Tomorrow? Same time?

Genevieve: Perfect! Thx!

Ariana moved between Zoey and Alex. "What's going on?"

Zoey put her hand on Ari's shoulder. "Sorry, sweetie. They need to reschedule for tomorrow."

Ariana sighed dramatically. "Oh, man! I really wanted to see her. Well, I guess that gives me more time to work on my project today. I have to work on a couple of the graphs and do some more painting."

"Ari, can you come here?" Alyssa called from the kitchen.

"Coming, Grandma!" Ariana raced over.

Alex took Zoey's hand. "Are you okay? You seem... I don't know. Not quite yourself."

She shrugged. "I'm getting by."

He arched an eyebrow. "Getting by?"

"Yeah. Some days are harder than others. You know how it is." She hoped he'd think she was referring to the abduction.

"Unfortunately." He laced his fingers through hers and led her down the stairs.

Zoey's stomach twisted, churned acid, and lurched. They were going to talk. Today. She was going to have to tell him the truth.

No more putting it off.

How would he react? Would he be disgusted by her? Could he accept her decision to have the baby? Would he be angry that she'd kept it from him?

Tears stung her eyes. She couldn't handle losing him again. What if he wanted to look into other pregnancy options? Or adoption? Would she change her mind to keep the only person she'd ever truly been in love with?

Time seemed to move in slow motion as they made their way down the stairs and outside.

Neither spoke as they crossed the yard and sat on a bench Chad had recently built underneath a large Japanese maple tree.

Alex put his hands on her shoulders and massaged, not saying a word.

Zoey's mind raced. Her heart thundered so loudly, she was sure Alex could hear it. She could hardly hear anything else over the noise.

He continued rubbing her shoulders for a few minutes before wrapping an arm around her. "Are you sure everything's okay? You haven't seemed yourself in a while."

"I'm dealing with an abduction!" Zoey snapped. "Sorry."

Alex kissed her temple. "You can talk to me, you know. I've been through that, too. It messes with the mind big time. But you're one of the strongest people I know, Zo. If anyone can put that behind them, it's you."

Tears threatened again. She swallowed. "It's more than that."

"More?" He tilted his head, and his eyes filled with concern. "What do you mean?"

This was it. The moment of truth. She would soon find out if she and Alex would remain engaged. If they would live the rest of their lives together.

"Zo?" He pulled some hair away from her face and held her gaze.

Her heart really was going to explode out of her chest.

"You can tell me anything."

Zoey's lips trembled. She looked down at her lap and sucked in a deep breath. There was no point in trying to put it off any longer. She looked up and met his gaze. "Alex, he raped me."

SHOCK

Alex stared at Zoey, trying to take in what she'd just said. He had to have misheard her. He *had* to have. It couldn't be true. It felt like a punch in the gut.

But the tears shining in her eyes and the fearful expression told him he hadn't heard wrong.

He finally found his voice. "He raped you?"

She nodded and wiped her eyes.

Alex's mind raced with more questions than he could spit out. He settled on one. "Why didn't you tell me sooner?"

Zoey buried her face against his chest and mumbled something he couldn't understand.

He clung to her. "Are you okay? Did you at least tell the doctors when you were in the hospital?"

She nodded. "They know. I'm going to have to testify about it when he goes to trial."

He kissed the top of her head. Again and again. A range of emotions swirled around—everything from heartbreak to anger. "I'm so sorry. So, so sorry. I should've been there to protect you!"

Zoey sat back and stared at him with a tear-streaked face. "There's more."

Alex reached for her hand but missed. His own hands were shaking out of control. His entire body was cold. Rage was building inside. He wanted to find a way into the county jail and beat the life out of that man. Even if it meant Alex would spend the rest of *his* days behind bars.

"Alex?"

He turned back to Zoey.

"There's something else I need to tell you."

"Okay." He took a deep breath. "What is it?"

Silence rested between them for a few minutes before she spoke. Tears spilled onto her face. "I'm pregnant."

He just stared at her. He tried to process the news. "You're…" He couldn't bring himself to say it. "And it's his?"

Zoey blinked, spilling more tears. Then she nodded. "I wish with everything in me that it wasn't. All I've wanted was to have more children with *you*. I hate him for stealing that from us! I *hate* him!"

Alex clenched his fists. "And *I* hate him for what he did to you! If I could get my hands on him…" He imagined himself torturing Dave slowly until he begged for death. Then denying him.

"Alex?"

He pushed the image from his mind and focused on his beautiful, hurting fiancée. "We'll get through this together. I'm not letting you deal with this alone for a moment longer. I only wish I'd insisted on finding out what was bothering you. I just chalked it up to dealing with the abduction."

Zoey frowned. "I doubt I would've told you before. I've been trying to ignore it, but it isn't something that can be ignored." She rubbed her belly.

He reached for her. "May I?"

She nodded.

Alex couldn't hide his surprise at how round her stomach was. "I'm definitely growing faster this time around."

"When was the last time you saw a doctor?"

"At the hospital."

He gave her a double-take. "That long? We need to get you in. Make sure you're doing okay."

"I am. Just tired. I've been taking all the supplements I'm supposed to and eating as best I can—when I can."

"I can't believe you've been dealing with all this on your own, Zo." He pulled her close and held onto her, trying to calm the storm raging inside of him. "No more of that, okay? We're a team. I'm here for you. There's nothing you have to face alone anymore. Not this, not anything."

She clung to him, shaking. "You don't hate me?"

"Hate you?" Alex exclaimed. "How could I ever hate you?"

Zoey mumbled something, but he couldn't understand with her face pressed against his chest.

"One thing you need to understand," he said. "I could never hate you. Not ever. I'm the luckiest man on earth to be marrying you."

She pulled back and wiped her eyes. "Even with this? I'm damaged goods. I'm carrying another man's baby."

"It's not your fault—and *no*, you're not damaged goods. Don't say it, don't think it, and don't believe it. It's not true. We'll work through all of this."

"How?"

If his mind spun any faster, he'd fall off the bench. "I don't know yet. We've already been through so much. We'll figure this out, too. You're not going to get rid of me that easily."

She threw her arms around him and sobbed. He rubbed her back and kissed the top of her head. Tears of his own threatened, and a lump in his throat was growing by the moment. It was all so much to take in, but more than anything, he wanted to take care of Zoey.

He couldn't think about what Dave had done to her. Not yet. She'd kept this to herself the entire time since it had happened, and that had to have been a horrible burden on top of everything she was going through with the pregnancy.

Zoey pulled away again and wiped away tears. "What are we going to do?"

"I'm going to take care of you. What do you need? Rest? Food? Something else?"

"I don't know. I really don't know."

Alex studied her. She looked beyond exhausted. More than him, actually. Dark circles under her eyes. Pale. Stress lines around her eyes. She looked like she was carrying an impossible weight.

He took her hand in his. "How about this? I take you home, then you get into your most comfortable clothes and pick out a movie while I run to the store for some lunch and ridiculous amounts of ice cream and pickles."

"Are you for real?"

Alex leaned over and kissed her cheek. "Of course. What else do you need? Those pregnancy vitamins? Something else I haven't thought of?"

He strained to think of other things she'd needed when pregnant with Ariana, but it was hard to remember. It felt like a lifetime ago—he'd only been fourteen and fifteen during her pregnancy, and besides that, her parents had been taking care of her then.

"You mean prenatal vitamins. Yeah, I'm taking those. Other supplements, too. I think I just need rest and you. You don't have to go to the store."

Alex kissed her again. "Do you have ice cream, pickles, and food for lunch?"

"I have plenty of food, but no ice cream or pickles."

"Then I'm going to the store. Let's go inside and let Ari know you aren't feeling good, then we'll get you home."

"I can drive. My car's over there."

"You can leave it here. I'll bring you back here later to get it."

She sniffled and wiped her eyes. "It's okay. I'll drive myself, Alex. I'm not helpless."

"Believe me, I know that." He gave her another kiss. "I just want to take away as much of that burden you've been carrying by yourself all this time."

CASES

Nick flipped through the pages in the old case file and moved over to the computer screen. He hated being at work on the weekend, but the kids had been happy enough to go to his parents' house for a few hours. Hopefully, that was all it would be. He didn't want to be working into the night.

His main focus for now was hunting down the parents of the twins Genevieve had found. It was like they'd vanished after the girls disappeared.

Not that he could blame them. The media could be like vultures, never leaving their prey alone. After experiencing such a monumental loss, they probably wanted to get away where nobody could find them. Possibly even going as far as changing their identities. They wouldn't be the first.

He felt for them, but it made his job harder. If he couldn't find anything, he'd have to pull in someone else from the case to help. Garcia had a way with these things. He was good at digging and reading people. That was probably how he'd picked up on something between Nick and Genevieve before anyone else.

Nick rubbed his eyes and went over the old files again, looking for a clue to where they might've gone. They'd been a local family, living not too far away from the burial house at the time.

It was too soon to say with so many victims still unidentified, but the killer had probably only taken a few of his victims from the area. There weren't many kids reported missing, especially still unsolved, from thirty years earlier.

They'd found a handful, but nothing to give anyone any idea that there had been a serial killer under their noses the whole time.

That meant the killer had to have gone out of the area and brought them back to the house in order to stay off the radar.

A chill ran down Nick's back. That was exactly what another recent killer had done. Flynn Myer, who had abducted Ariana and very nearly killed her, had gotten his yearly victims from various areas throughout the Northwest.

He was the same man Alex swore was still running loose and would stake his life on it, if given the chance. Nick had checked into it himself, and Myer was most certainly in the state's most notorious prison on death row. He wasn't running around stalking Alex.

Nick had even looked into the convenience store where Alex had seen a guy he claimed was Flynn. But the station had burned down, and with it, any video surveillance.

But here they were with a strikingly similar killer—someone who appeared to kill girls of about the same age for close to as many years as Myer had. It was uncertain if other details matched. At least until more victims were identified.

Did these crimes take place randomly throughout the year, unlike Myer's whose were all killed around Halloween? Had these victims been sexually assaulted? If so, that would also be different. Myer had been twisted in many ways, but he'd never harmed any of his victims in that way.

Nick shook his head. Why was he thinking about Flynn Myer?

The man was in prison. He dropped his victims in bodies of water. These remains were all buried. Not the same killer.

He needed to find the twins' parents. That was what he had to focus on doing. After all these years, they deserved closure.

Nick shoved his thoughts aside and combed through the old files with a critical eye. Looking for something. Anything. A clue that had to have been missed along the way. Something that might stand out now in light of recent events.

Then he saw it. Scrawled in a note near the back. The family had a vacation home not far away. Relatives near there.

He reached for his coffee mug. Empty.

His legs needed stretching, anyway. He'd been staring at fading ink too long.

The only sounds outside his office were of keyboards typing. Not many were in the office at this hour. It was a critical case for sure, since they were trying to find a serial killer, but with nobody's life on the line, it wasn't as urgent. People could go home and sleep. At least until they discovered a missing child matching this sicko's MO.

Then they'd be looking at more sleepless nights. Plenty of them.

Nick actually wouldn't mind being on one of those cases again. He'd been too close to the victims the last two times to participate.

"You're still here, Captain?" Garcia asked.

Nick filled his mug. "I'm getting close to finding the twins' parents. I want to give them closure before the night's over."

"Whatcha got? Maybe I can help."

"Be my guest." Nick filled him in, then showed him the file in his office.

Garcia came back with his laptop and his fingers flew across the keyboard fast enough to set it on fire.

"Yeah, right here. Looks like both parents are using their

middle names as first names. It's probably just what they needed to keep the media off their backs."

"You want to come with me to give them the news?"

Garcia nodded. "Let me grab a couple things and let Mackey know where I'm going. She's helping me look into some cold cases that could be related."

"Sure. Meet you at my car." Nick closed down his computer and gathered what he needed before heading to his Mustang.

"Don't you ever use the cruisers?" Garcia sat and buckled in. "You could save on gas, you know."

"I like to feel undercover. Besides, I can write off the miles at tax time."

"I'd rather just save on the gas."

They discussed the case for most of the ninety-minute drive. Just as Nick was pulling off the freeway, both of their phones made noises.

"What is it?" Nick asked.

Garcia looked at his screen. "They've ID'd one of the recent vics. Missing girl from Boise. Reported three months ago. Dental records are a perfect match."

Nick squeezed the wheel. "I wonder how many of our vics are from out of the area."

And if there were more similarities to Myer's MO.

OPPORTUNITY

Tony crouched behind a shrub as the jogger passed by, engrossed by whatever played in her earbuds. She didn't even notice him, inches from her legs.

Across the street in her yard, Maisie rode in her shiny new pink toy Hummer. Its engine was nearly as loud as its real counterpart.

So far, the little girl stayed in the grass, but she kept inching closer to the sidewalk. She was eyeing the concrete like it was a prize to be had.

Her dad was in the garage, tinkering with a motorcycle. Every so often, Maisie's mom came to make sure he was watching their daughter. He was paying more attention to the bike.

Patience. It would pay off sooner or later.

It almost always did.

The fact that it sometimes didn't pay off made the whole thing all the more thrilling. If it were easy, it wouldn't be a challenge. His heart wouldn't be racing like it was right that moment.

Maisie's dad went deeper into the garage, hidden by a car. The little girl herself moved closer to the sidewalk. The toy Hummer's wheels went halfway over the cement this time.

It was getting close to time. Soon he would talk to Maisie again. Maybe convince her to come for the present. Or maybe just build more trust. It might take a few days.

Patience. That was all it would take. Then all his hard work would pay off.

Her dad reappeared, tools in hand and got back to work on the motorcycle, turning his back to the yard and his daughter.

The miniature Hummer now pulled off the grass entirely and rode over the sidewalk as she circled back to the yard.

Her dad didn't even notice.

Maisie continued widening her path until she rode up and down the sidewalk, not even bothering with her yard except to turn around. There was no reason, not when her dad was so engrossed with the motorcycle and the mom hadn't come out in a while.

At first, she stayed directly in front of her house, not crossing the clear lines marking the edges of her property—longer grass on both sides indicated where Maisie's yard ended and the neighbors' began. But then she began inching closer and closer each time she turned around until she was crossing over on the neighbors' yards.

Her dad turned around when she rode on the driveway. "You're supposed to stay on the grass."

"This is more fun."

"Your mom wouldn't like it."

"Please," Maisie begged.

He frowned. "Just don't go in the road."

"Yay!" She tore down the driveway and to the sidewalk, barreling down past the property line.

Maisie was heading away from Tony, but she turned around in the neighbor's yard soon enough and flew past her house again, squealing and giggling.

Her dad didn't turn around, nor did her mom so much as peek outside.

Maisie passed the next house and didn't slow as she went past another house and another.

It was time for him to make a move. He looked around for anyone who might be looking his way.

Nobody was.

He rose and stretched his legs. The road was quiet, other than the sounds of the toy Hummer's engine and of the hammering from Maisie's garage. Her dad was completely engrossed with the motorcycle.

Maisie turned around and headed back toward her house.

The front door swung open.

Tony ducked back behind the shrub.

Maisie's mom appeared. "Maisie!"

"She's riding on the sidewalk." Maisie's dad didn't look away from his project.

"I don't want her on the street," the mom objected.

"She's on the sidewalk. I'm watching her."

The mom crossed her arms and stepped into the yard, watching Maisie.

The little girl waved as she passed in front of the yard. "Daddy said I could ride out here!"

Her mom scowled but didn't object. She watched as her daughter went up and down the sidewalk a few times, then turned to her husband. "You're not watching her if your back is to her."

"I can hear her!"

"If anything happens to her, it's on you. Just know that."

"She's *fine*."

Maisie's mom glared at him. "I have to get back inside. I wish you'd watch her."

"Our neighborhood is perfectly safe, and I *am* watching her. I can hear her just fine."

They had a few more words, before the wife stormed back into the house, muttering to herself then slamming the door.

Meanwhile, Maisie continued her path up and down the sidewalk, traveling a little farther each time.

Tony waited a minute, then rose to his feet again and strolled inconspicuously in the direction of his car with the present inside. He just needed to cross the street to reach it now.

Maisie was inches from it, her blonde hair flying behind her.

He crossed the street and checked to make sure his car was unlocked as he passed it. It was. The balloon and present were all in the backseat, eager to leave and have Maisie join them.

She turned around, now five houses away from her own.

The man waved and leaned against his car as she neared.

It took a moment for recognition to cover her face. She waved back and then zoomed past, barreling toward her house and passing it.

He didn't move from his spot, though he was ready to jump out of sight the moment one of Maisie's parents showed up at the edge of their property.

They didn't.

Maisie went pretty far away before finally turning around and heading back his way.

"Come inside, Maisie!" Her mom's voice drifted his way.

The little girl waved as she rode past her yard and neared him again.

"We need to go meet Grandma and Grandpa! Put that truck away, Maisie!"

Tony swore under his breath. So much for his big opportunity. He'd been so close.

Patience, he reminded himself. There would always be tomorrow. Or the next day, or the day after that. Each day was a new opportunity to make himself more familiar to the girl. To finally bring her to his cabin.

He opened the back passenger door and pulled out the pink balloon.

Maisie slowed as she approached, a questioning expression slowly crossing her face.

The man handed it to her. "Here, have this before it stops floating. Happy birthday, Maisie."

She grasped it, her eyes wide. "Thanks, mister."

"Tony." He smiled widely. "You'd better get back to your mom before you get in trouble. Go on."

Maisie managed to turn around and barrel down the sidewalk without letting go of the string.

He watched until she turned onto her yard and disappeared from sight. Then he got into his car and drove away, already making plans for next time.

DOUBTS

Genevieve paced the condo, unable to stop staring at the door.

"Would you sit down?" Her mom glared at her.

"No! Where is dad?"

Mom sighed. "Fishing. You know that's how he deals with stress."

Genevieve shook her head. "He can't do this! Not when there's an active police investigation. He's making it hard on those trying to prove his innocence."

"The truth always prevails." Mom turned back to her crossword puzzle.

And that was exactly what was starting to worry Genevieve. Could her dad actually be the killer? She hated to think that, but he didn't leave her any reason not to. If he wasn't guilty, why would he disappear like he had been? All it did was make him look suspicious.

She continued pacing. If she, his daughter, suspected him, then how much more did those working on the case?

They were already giving him the benefit of the doubt because of his relation to Genevieve, but that could only go so far. As her mom had pointed out, they needed to get to the truth, and soon. Every minute the serial killer ran free, young girls remained at risk.

"You're driving me crazy." Mom gathered her pen and crossword puzzle. "I'm going to bed. Tell Dad he can wake me when he gets home."

Genevieve nodded. She didn't say anything as her mom made her way to the master bedroom. She only continued pacing, now stopping each time she passed the window facing the parking lot.

"Where are you, Dad?"

She checked her phone for any calls or texts. Nothing from anyone.

After more pacing, she checked on Tinsley. The girl snored from the bed.

Genevieve would love to be able to sleep so soundly. Ever since all this had started, she had been sleeping fitfully, waking often.

It felt like it had been at least a week, but it had only been two days. Two days since this whole mess started.

How was that possible?

She went back to the living room, leaving Tinsley's door open just a crack. After some more pacing, she finally plopped down on the futon and scrolled through the newsfeed on social media, distracting herself with cat videos and news around the world.

A serial killer had been caught on the East Coast after a flood had swept through a neighborhood and led authorities to the killer's lair in the basement.

Hopefully the murderer who was using her parents' backyard as a cemetery would be caught soon. And with any luck, it wouldn't be her dad. She could just hear the whispers if it did end up being him—the father of a police officer. People would ridicule her for not seeing the signs.

But there hadn't been any. Not until she and Tinsley had dug up the bones.

Stop!

She took a deep breath. Her dad wasn't a killer. The man was as loving and kind as they came, giving to a fault. He was just making some dumb decisions now. That was it. That, and Genevieve's wild imagination connecting unrelated dots.

She set her phone aside and closed her eyes. Exhaustion set in, squeezing every inch of her body. Her muscles ached. Even her skin burned.

The fog of sleep overcame her and she started to drift off, floating away from the living room. Darkness remained and her feet pressed onto the ground.

Genevieve looked around. She couldn't see much. A faint light came from the distance, way up in the sky. It was the moon, and it illuminated the tops of black spruce trees.

Woods. Not just any woods. *The* woods.

She recognized the path. It was the exact place where her life had nearly ended. Where she had been terrorized.

Pine cones and twigs crunched. Someone was coming her way.

Genevieve sat up, gasping for air.

It took a moment for her to realize she was in Nick's condo, far from the forest. Her tormentors were in jail. Ineligible for parole.

Her dad stood by the door, hanging up his jacket. "Didn't mean to wake you."

She took a deep breath and held it for a moment. Her whole body shook. "Where have you been?"

"Fishing."

"Dad, that has to stop. If you won't listen to me as your daughter, please listen to me as an officer of the law. No more fishing until all of this is over. When you go fishing by yourself, you have no alibi. You look guilty, no matter how innocent you are."

"I appreciate your concern, but it isn't necessary. Your mom knows this is how I deal with stress. So should you. I'm sticking close to home. Coming back here every night. Sometimes I travel and fish in Montana or Idaho for up to a week at a time. I'm not doing that now."

"You should be doing everything you can to prove your innocence. Right now, you're just giving the authorities reason to question you."

"The captain says he believes me." Dad gave her a look that clearly asked if she believed him, too.

She wanted to. More than anything. He was making it hard. Really hard.

"Just wait until this mess is behind us. That's all you need to do. I'm worried about you."

He lumbered into the living room and stood next to the futon, staring down at her. "Why don't you come with me tomorrow? You can see that I'm just fishing. It'll set your mind at ease. You can even be my alibi. All problems solved."

"You know I can't. I need to take care of Tinsley."

"We both know your mom will watch her. She'll be thrilled we're having father-daughter time."

Genevieve shook her head. "I'm not leaving her alone with Tinsley. With everything going on, Tinsley could have a meltdown. I don't want Mom having to deal with that on her own."

"Tinsley seems to be doing better than ever."

She jumped to her feet and glared at him. "How would you know? All you've been doing is fishing! If that's what you've actually been doing."

"You don't think I have been?"

"I wouldn't know. Nobody would."

"Your captain found me fishing. That isn't enough proof for you?"

"After hours of searching! After you wouldn't answer your phone."

Dad sighed. "We've been over this, Genevieve. I didn't hear it. Honest mistake. Do you want to accuse me of something?"

"I just don't want to see you wrongly imprisoned. It happens. Especially when people make themselves look guilty."

"I'm not."

"Dad, please consider finding a new way to de-stress yourself. That's all I'm asking. Something where there are lots of witnesses. Take up bowling. Get a pedicure. Anything with people around."

"A pedicure? You want me to have my fingernails painted?"

"That would be a manicure. No, lots of men get pedicures. They'll soak your feet, massage them, clip your nails. No colorful polish required. It'll be relaxing and there will be plenty of people around to see you."

"I'm no sissy. I'll stick with fishing. Goodnight, dear."

"Dad—"

He kissed her forehead and went to the master bedroom without another word.

COMFORT

~~~~

Alex lifted Zoey off the couch and carried her to the bedroom. Her head rolled onto his shoulder, but she didn't wake. They'd watched several movies and eaten tons of ice cream. He hadn't left her side except to get more snacks or to use the bathroom.

She had snuggled close to him, practically clinging to him the entire time. So unlike her. Zoey was the strongest, most independent woman he'd ever met.

It infuriated him that she'd been violated so badly that it had changed her. He was mad at himself for not seeing the signs earlier, but he'd attributed her jumpiness to the abduction. And with as busy and tired as he'd been with academy, he hadn't noticed she'd pulled away physically. But now looking back, he saw all the signs of her backing away from him.

He wanted to kick himself for not seeing anything sooner, but it would be pointless. At least he knew now. He could give her the comfort and protection she needed. The monster who had done this to her was behind bars, and he hadn't killed Zoey. She was still alive. That was something Alex was beyond grateful for.

He settled Zoey into the bed, tucking the covers around her.

She mumbled something but didn't wake. He brushed a few strands of hair from her face and kissed her temples.

He started to climb in next to her, but realized he wasn't sleepy even though he should have been. His mind wouldn't stop racing now that he knew just how brutally she had been violated.

Alex went out to the living room and found his phone on the coffee table. Two new texts.

Unknown: Flynn still wants to see you.

Unknown: He's waiting.

Anger ripped through Alex.

Alex: Who is this??

The little dancing dots showed the other person was responding.

Unknown: Doesn't matter.

Alex: Where is Flynn?

Unknown: You know.

Alex: Do I?

Unknown: Yes.

Alex: He wants me to visit him in prison?

Unknown: He really wants to talk to you.

Alex: Why?

Unknown: You gonna leave him hanging?

Alex: He deserves to hang.

Unknown: Funny. Not.

Alex: Who are you??

Unknown: None of your concern.

Alex: Why does Flynn want to see me?

Unknown: Why do you think?

Alex: When? Where?

Unknown: Soon. You know where.

He wanted to throw the phone across the room.

Alex: I'm gonna block you.

Unknown: I wouldn't do that.

Alex: Why not?

No response. No message, no dancing dots.

Alex: Hello?

Nothing.

Now he really wanted to chuck the phone. He waited a full minute before heading into the bedroom.

What he needed to do was to stop engaging the unknown texter. He was probably doing exactly what he wanted. For all he knew, the texter was just messing with him. Had no connection to Flynn, whether in jail or not. Alex had three priorities—Zoey, Ariana, and the academy. None of those involved Flynn, other than the fact that Flynn had abducted Ariana and was now supposedly locked up for it and for killing the other girls.

But if he wasn't... then he *was* Alex's concern. And he'd definitely seen Flynn several times since he was supposed to be in prison—at the funeral, at the middle school, and at the convenience store. He was either getting in and out of a maximum security facility or someone was in there in his place.

He held his thumb over the button to block the mystery person, but then didn't press it. Instead, he stuffed the phone into his pocket and tiptoed into Zoey's room.

Alex climbed into the bed, careful not to wake her, then pulled her close. She mumbled something but didn't wake.

He lay there, kissing the top of her head every so often and letting his mind run.

After a while, Zoey tossed and turned, pushing the blankets off. Alex pulled them up over her, but she twisted out of them again, still sleeping.

He gave up and decided to cover her after she fell into a deeper sleep. She rolled onto her side, and the curve of her stomach became more profound.

Alex stared at it, a heaviness squeezing his chest. He hated that someone else's baby was growing inside of her. More than that, he hated how it had gotten there.

A mixture of emotions ran through him, some irrational and

some rational—jealousy, fury, fear, doubt, and a few others he couldn't identify.

He wanted nothing more than to spend the rest of his life with Zoey. That was all he'd ever wanted. He hated Dave for what he'd done to not only Zoey, but their dreams.

TALKING

⁂

Nick pulled the cinnamon rolls from the oven and placed them on top of the stove.

"Are they ready?" Hanna jumped around behind him. "They smell so good!"

"They need to cool." He closed the oven and slid off the mitts. "You can help me frost them in a few minutes if you'd like."

"Yay!" She danced around the kitchen, clapping and singing.

Nick opened the fridge and pulled out the bowl of fruit he'd cut up a few minutes earlier. "Can you see if Ava and Parker are up yet?"

"Can I wake them if they're not?" Hanna pleaded with her eyes.

"Just let them sleep."

"Aw." Her shoulders slumped as she plodded down the hallway.

"Just check," he reminded her as he pulled the freshly-squeezed juice from the fridge. He set it and the fruit on the dining room table before going back to check on the cinnamon rolls.

Hanna came back with a slight frown. "Still sleeping. Sure I can't wake them? Ava kept me up last night."

Nick arched a brow. "She did? Doing what?"

"Talking. Probably on her phone to Braylon." Hanna added an extra syllable to her sister's boyfriend's name.

"How late?"

Hanna shrugged. "Dunno. Can I frost those now?"

Nick tried to remember if he could hear anything the night before, but he'd been so tired he likely could have slept through an explosion.

"Daddy?"

He took a peek at the rolls. "They're probably ready. Remember how to spread it?"

She nodded vigorously and reached for the packet of icing.

Nick cut the top off and handed it to her. As she squeezed it out, he finished getting the table ready for breakfast with Genevieve, Tinsley, and his kids.

Ding-dong.

Perfect timing. He checked his reflection in a mirror by the door—he had Corrine to thank for the placement. There wasn't much he could thank her for, but she did have interior decorating smarts.

Nick reached for the doorknob, but Hanna swooped in and pulled it open. "Tinsley!"

The two girls hugged, then ran down the hall toward Hanna's room. Two distinct voices sounded.

His eyes widened. "Tinsley just said something to Hanna."

"I know." Genevieve smiled as she stepped in, and they exchanged a pleased expression. "I've never heard her speak more than she has in the last few days."

Nick took the covered plate from her and nudged the door closed. "That's great news."

"It's odd timing, but I'll take it." She glanced at the table. "This looks great. Can I help with anything?"

"No, everything's ready. It's just a matter of dragging the kids out here."

Nick called the kids. Hanna and Tinsley rushed out and sat

down at the table. Nick knocked on Parker's and Ava's doors. "Breakfast is ready! Genevieve and Tinsley are here."

He went to the table and sat. Just as he was about to tell the others to eat, Parker and Ava plodded into the dining room.

"You guys look like zombies." Hanna giggled, and Tinsley joined in.

"Ha-ha." Ava glared at her sister and said good morning to Genevieve. She then went into the kitchen and made herself a cup of coffee.

Hanna poked at the covered dish Genevieve brought. "What did you make?"

"Hash browns. You like them?"

"They're my favorite! Especially with lots of ketchup."

It didn't take long for the food to disappear, then for the kids to run off in different directions. Music played in Parker's room and the shower started in the bathroom. The back door slammed shut as Hanna and Tinsley headed for the backyard.

"Want some help cleaning this mess?" Genevieve asked.

Nick took her hand and rubbed his thumb along her wrist. "Maybe in a bit. How are you doing?"

"Tired but okay, considering."

"I know that feeling all too well. How are your parents holding up?"

She frowned and her expression showed just how exhausted she was. "Dad keeps fishing like the lakes are running out of fish. He leaves Mom to deal with the stress on her own. I guess he thinks I'm going to take care of her."

"Is that typical?" Nick continued rubbing her wrist.

"Unfortunately. I feel like this is overboard, but then again, so is the whole situation. What are the chances we'd live in a house that's used as a burial ground? I'm sure he just doesn't know how to handle everything. He certainly isn't going to talk about it with anyone. So, he fishes. Every day now, apparently. Must be nice to be retired."

"Everybody has their own ways of dealing with stress. Look at Tinsley. She hasn't been talking to anyone, either."

"Yeah, but she's a kid and she's been through so much worse. Losing her parents like that. Having to help her mom kidnap and torture people." Genevieve shuddered and her eyes took on a glassy look.

Nick pulled her into his embrace. "How are *you* holding up under all the stress?"

She laced her smooth fingers through his. "Trying to be strong for everyone else."

He ran his palm over her hair, kissed the top of her head, and took in the fruity smell of her shampoo. "You don't have to be strong for me."

Genevieve relaxed a little against him but didn't say anything.

Nick smoothed her hair. "I obviously don't know exactly what you're going through, but I know what it's like to be on that side of an investigation. To be unable to do anything professionally and to watch people you care about dealing with impossible situations."

She nodded. "How are the kids handling Corrine's incarceration?"

He took in a deep breath. "It's hard on them. I can see it in their eyes whenever they talk about her. Hanna's the only one who actually expresses her sadness to me. She's young enough that she isn't self-conscious about crying. Parker just gets mad, and Ava..." Nick had a hard time finding words to describe how his oldest was handling everything. "I think she's using avoidance as her tool of choice. She spends a lot of time with her friends and boyfriend, which I think is good. She's even taking an interest in tennis, which I'd have never expected, but then again Braylon is on the school team."

"Sounds healthy enough to me. I'd be worried if she was hiding out in her room, avoiding everyone."

"That's true. None of the kids are doing that."

"At least you care."

Nick paused. "What do you mean?"

Genevieve hesitated. "I went through something as a teenager, but nobody paid any attention to how I dealt with it once it was over."

"You went through something? What was it?" He raked his mind, trying to remember if she had mentioned something before, but couldn't think of anything.

She shook in his arms.

"Are you okay?" He held her closer. "You don't have to talk about it if you don't want to. I didn't mean to pry."

"I do want to talk about it." Her voice wavered. "I haven't since it happened."

Nick's mind pulled a bunch of different theories—and some were horrific, given what he'd seen in his years on the force. "I'm not going anywhere."

Her hand tightened and shook in his, and she drew in a deep breath. She started to say something, but stopped.

He rubbed her wrist again. "I would never judge you. Never think less of you. You're one of the most amazing people I've ever met. One of the strongest and most intelligent officers on the force."

She brought her hand up to her face and when she pulled it away, a tear rolled down to her arm.

Nick's chest tightened. He hated to see her hurting.

Genevieve nestled closer to him and sniffled. "When I was sixteen, I went with a friend to her cousins' house out in the country. Some small town I can't even remember the name of that was surrounded by woods."

He continued rubbing her wrist and he kissed the top of her head every so often, waiting for her to continue.

"Her cousins were a little older. Graduated high school and had their own little house. It was rundown, but I didn't think anything of it because I figured they just had a hard time making ends meet at their age. But then I found out later they were into drugs and some weird cult-like stuff. Anyway, late that night they woke us up because they wanted to go into the woods for a bonfire. I should've known something was off when they all grabbed long hooded robes…"

RELIVE

Genevieve shivered as the memory of that night flooded her mind, making her feel like she was right back in that rundown house. She could smell the odors, which she now knew were various drugs.

She had given a concerned look to her friend, Chelsea.

Chelsea had just shrugged and grabbed her coat. She seemed to think a bonfire in the woods would be fun. An adventure.

Since Chelsea wasn't worried, Genevieve ignored her instincts trying to warn her that something was wrong. She stupidly trusted her friend over herself.

They piled into a van. Between the seats lay all kinds of medieval-like weaponry instead of what she would've expected for a bonfire. No marshmallows or roasting sticks.

Her skin prickled, but she ignored it and laughed with Chelsea and her cousins over some stupid hunting story one of them told.

The van roared to life, then backfired loudly. They drove down a bumpy road and into the forest until the trail ended.

Genevieve had expected everyone to pile out and start the bonfire within sight of the vehicle. Instead, they all grabbed weapons and supplies, then headed down a narrow trail for what felt like an hour. They weaved between trees, only able to see as far as the flashlights allowed. She didn't have one.

By the time they finally stopped, every muscle in her body burned. She had been in decent shape but wasn't dressed for a hike, wearing sandals on her feet which had made some painful blisters on her soles and heels over the trek.

Before long, a huge fire roared, the flames licking toward the nearby tree branches. Five or six other junkies joined the group. Everyone other than Genevieve slipped on a robe.

Including Chelsea.

They all had sharp weapons. The mood shifted in an instant.

Genevieve's heart nearly exploded out of her chest. It had been a setup. For what, she didn't know yet. But everyone else was in on something.

She had to get away. Immediately.

But everyone was staring at her. They stepped closer, surrounding her. Not giving her a chance for escape.

Why hadn't she listened to her instincts? Would that be the last mistake she ever made? Would she ever see her parents again? Her friends? Boyfriend? Graduate high school?

Images from her life raced through her mind, everything from early memories to recent ones. She'd had a fight with her best friend Brittney that afternoon. They hadn't made up. What if that was their last conversation ever?

Someone grabbed Genevieve's arms and yanked hard. She stumbled and gasped for air. Looked for Chelsea in the crowd. Everyone looked the same in the hoods and darkness.

One person shouted something that made no sense. Everyone else responded, also not making any sense. They repeated the same line over and over.

Chanting. They were chanting. The person holding her tightened his grip on her arms, digging his fingertips into her flesh. That would bruise. So much for wearing that sleeveless dress for her date the next night. If she even made it.

All the robed figures lined up and marched around the fire. The guy holding her took large steps, making it hard for her to keep up without falling. Every time she stumbled, he dug his fingers tighter into her arms. It felt like he was digging right into the muscle.

The chanting grew louder. The circle moved faster. It was hard to breathe.

She struggled to free herself, but only earned herself more pain in her flesh. Then the guy wrapped his foot around her leg and let go of her arms.

Genevieve fell to the ground, scraping her face on a jagged rock and knocking the wind out of her lungs. The chanting grew even louder. She tried to get up.

People stepped on her. Feet dug into her back, her arms, her legs. Someone even stepped on her face. A pebble stuck in the bottom of the shoe sliced her skin.

She cried out, but couldn't even hear herself. Nobody was going to help her. She was in the middle of some woods she didn't know. Her car was miles away at Chelsea's house. She'd left her phone back at the cousin's shack.

Even if she could get away, that would only be the beginning. Getting home would be next to impossible. If she could even find her way back out of the woods.

But she had to try. If she didn't, she was giving up already.

She struggled to get up, despite the parade of feet stomping on her. A foot stepped on her fingers. Pain shot from her middle finger and radiated out.

Genevieve twisted and turned, managing to avoid the feet. She jumped up and fled the circle, ignoring the pains ripping through her.

Must. Get. Away.

Someone pulled on her hair, yanking her head back.

She yelled, not that it did any good over the chants and crackling fire.

The cloaked figure pulled her closer and wrapped an arm around her chest, forcing her against him. She turned and bit down as hard as she could while at the same time kicking backward, aiming for his knees.

He cried out, then shoved her toward the ground. She tried to catch herself, but crashed against a prickly bush.

Hands yanked her back. Someone forced her back to the ground while another person yanked off her hoodie. The zipper scratched along her face and twigs dug into her flesh, her arms now fully exposed since she was only wearing a tank top.

A hooded figure forced her onto her back and straddled her while two others held her arms and shoulders down.

Genevieve screamed so loud it made her throat hurt. Not that it made any difference. She could barely hear herself, but that didn't stop someone from pressing his nicotine-smelling hand over her mouth.

She squirmed and tried biting, struggling to free herself from the impossible situation. Whatever they planned to do to her, she wasn't going to make it easy. They underestimated her if they thought she'd give up before she lost consciousness.

The hand covering her mouth moved closer to her nose until it pressed against her nostrils, blocking the air.

She couldn't breathe!

Genevieve fought harder than ever. Not that it did much good. Rocks and twigs dug into her flesh while the hands holding her down applied more pressure. Someone struck her cheek. Spit sprayed across her face.

Everything faded into darkness.

CONNECTION

Nick tried to remain calm. His chest tightened and a lump formed in his throat.

Genevieve sobbed in his arms, shaking and cold. He pulled her onto his lap, rubbing her back and trying to kiss away her tears. But there was nothing he could do to take away what had happened to her.

It was nothing short of a miracle that she'd survived the attack. He wanted to ask how she'd gotten away. Where she'd woken up. What those bastards had done to her after she'd blacked out.

Instead, he just held her and let her weep. It was all he could do to keep from crying along with her, but he needed to be strong for her.

Ava walked past, dressed and with her hair styled and full face of makeup. She arched a brow at Nick.

He waved her away.

She mouthed, "Going to Braylon's."

Nick nodded. Normally, he'd double-check that her boyfriend's parents would be home, but he'd deal with that later. Ava knew the rules. And the consequences of breaking said rules.

She hurried outside, and Genevieve didn't seem to notice the distraction.

Nick comforted her as best he could while fighting his own tears, until she finally gasped for air and rubbed her eyes. She'd cried away her eye makeup. She looked so vulnerable.

It suffocated him. He struggled to breathe.

He found his voice. "When did you wake up?"

Genevieve swallowed. "Light was starting to shine through the trees but it was still pretty dark." Her voice was shaky. "The bonfire had burned out and nobody was in sight. Not even Chelsea. I didn't know if they'd left me for dead. With as badly as I hurt, it seemed likely."

Nick cupped her chin and stared into her beautiful gray eyes. "You're the strongest person I've ever met."

She frowned. "I'm only strong because I have to be. What other choice do I have after enduring that?"

"Not many people would choose to become an officer and face people like your attackers every day."

Her expression intensified. "I want to serve justice."

"Understandable." Nick cleared his throat. "How did you get home?"

Genevieve twisted a strand of hair around her finger and tears shone in her eyes again.

"I'm sorry, I shouldn't have asked."

"No, it's okay. I actually…" She took a deep breath. "It's good to talk about, even though it's hard. Thank you for listening."

He kissed her forehead. "Think nothing of it."

She held his gaze for a moment before speaking. "I got up and ran. Everything hurt, but at least I had my sandals. I have no idea how long I ran. The sun was high in the sky by the time I came to a small stream. I was thirsty and hungry and desperate. The water was clear, so I drank it and I washed myself off, not knowing anything about washing away evidence."

Nick's stomach tightened. He wanted to ask what evidence exactly, but if she didn't want to talk about the specific injuries, he wasn't going to push it. He was certain he knew the answer, even without her saying a word.

Genevieve played with a nail before continuing. "Once I dried off, I kept going in the same direction as best I could with the thick trees blocking my way every so often. It was almost dark by the time I broke free of the woods. I didn't know where I was, but I managed to flag down a car. Luckily, it was an off-duty officer, so I was in good hands. She drove me directly to the nearest hospital."

"What happened to your attackers?"

"They ended up in jail. Even Chelsea. Turns out they were more than happy to snitch on each other to reduce their sentences. But then later it was discovered they'd actually murdered some people. I was lucky. None of them are ever supposed to get out because of the murder charges. That's what allows me to sleep at night."

Nick pulled her close. "I had no idea you'd gone through all of that."

"It's not something I like to advertise. Like I said, I haven't told anyone else."

"Your parents know, don't they?"

She cleared her throat. "Some. They don't know most of what happened. I didn't want them listening when I gave my testimony in court, so they didn't. Basically, I tried to downplay it as much as I could."

"So, you've been dealing with this on your own for all this time?"

Genevieve nodded.

"Those days are over. Any time you want to talk or cry or yell, give me a call. I don't care what time it is. Two in the morning or the middle of a work day, I'll stop what I'm doing."

She sat back and stared at him with wide eyes. "Really?"

He nodded. "I'm serious. Just say the word."

She wrapped her arms around him and nestled against him. "You don't know how much that means to me."

CLOSER

Tony leaned to the side to pass the offering plate to Gayle, who gave him a stiff smile before passing it onto the next person. Church was the last place Gayle had wanted to come, but since she and Tony hadn't spent much time together lately, his girlfriend agreed most reluctantly.

"What's the deal?" she whispered. "You feeling the need for repentance or something?"

"Shh. I'm listening to the song. You didn't have to come with me."

"Would I have seen you otherwise?"

He shrugged and kept his gaze to the front of the sanctuary, pretending to focus on the solo performance. His gaze was actually on Maisie's parents a few rows up.

They sat next to each other with just enough space between them to make Tony think they weren't happy with each other. Were they arguing about the balloon Maisie had come home with the night before while riding her little Hummer up and down the sidewalk? He hadn't meant to cause friction. Okay, yes he had. He really had.

"What are you grinning about?" Gayle nudged him.

"Am I grinning?" He tried to stop, but couldn't. Not when Maisie's parents were so upset over the balloon.

"Seriously, why?" Gayle asked.

"Because it's a lovely song," he lied.

Gayle scowled. "Since when do you use words like *lovely*?"

"Would you just listen to the music? It's a time for reflection."

She muttered something but stayed quiet.

Good. He hated it when women wouldn't listen. And he didn't want to be in a bad mood when he saw Maisie soon. With any luck, the little girl seeing him with a woman would help set her mind at ease about him. Sometimes that helped.

Sometimes.

Maisie's parents didn't scoot closer or farther away from each other during the rest of the service. When everyone rose to sing, they kept their distance. They didn't hold hands or put an arm around each other like some other couples.

Tony put his arm around Gayle so as to keep up appearances. She moved closer to him. His was a small gesture, but it made a difference, whether it had any emotion behind it or not.

He kept his arm around her through the next song, and then removed it once the service was dismissed.

"Can we go?" Gayle threw him a petulant pout.

"We haven't met anyone yet."

Her shoulders slumped.

"Oh, stop."

Maisie's dad made his way down the aisle. Her mom remained at the pew, speaking with another woman.

"I'm hungry. Let's go and get something to eat. I'll buy if we go right now."

He furrowed his brow. "Stop whining, woman. I'll tell you when I'm ready to leave."

Gayle's expression pinched tight, then she stormed out of the sanctuary.

Oh, well. She'd get over it. And if not, no major loss. He'd have

Maisie soon enough. She was at just the right age when females were still sweet and agreeable. He didn't really need Gayle, anyway.

He took a deep breath and held onto the image of Maisie in his cabin as he made his way up the aisle, nodding at people as he passed. Maisie's mom was one of them, exiting the sanctuary before him.

Gayle stood by the door, her arms crossed. She glared at him.

He swallowed back a retort and smiled at her, keeping Maisie in mind. "Don't be upset. We'll leave soon enough, and I'll be happy to buy lunch. Let's meet some people first."

"Why?" Her tone held an annoying whine.

It was enough to make him want to slap her across the face. He didn't, of course. He pictured Maisie's sweet face and took Gayle's hand in his. "Because I'd like to meet some people. We'll leave soon, I promise. I'm hungry as well."

She sighed. "Fine. I don't want to be here all day. I have things to do."

"You didn't have to come, you know."

"I've hardly seen you at all lately, even though you work remotely."

"My boss kept me busy this week. He has a big deadline looming, so that means more work for me—whether I'm in the office or home."

"Even yesterday? On a Saturday?"

"You think my boss cares about me relaxing on the weekend? Come on. Stop bugging me. I get enough of that from him. I don't need it from you, too."

Her nostrils flared, but she kept quiet. Thankfully.

Maisie and her mom appeared from down a crowded corridor. The little girl grasped some colorful papers and talked excitedly, but her mom wasn't paying any attention.

How ungrateful. Maisie was trying to tell her mom something

important to her, and she didn't even care. The mother was basically grooming the girl to turn into a whiny, demanding woman.

He would put a stop to that.

Once he trained Maisie to stay sweet and innocent, he wouldn't need the Gayles of the world. He wouldn't need anyone else at all.

Maisie's mom stopped and spoke with a group of three other women. Their children all ran around the adults, chasing each other and giggling.

None of the moms seemed to notice until one of them told her son to take it outside. Several of the kids scrambled toward the door.

Maisie and one other kid asked their moms if it was okay.

The simple act sent a warm shiver down the man's spine. He'd definitely set his sights on the right girl. So sweet, so obedient. Maybe not so much with the Hummer, inching toward the sidewalk. But that was something they could work on in the cabin.

Maisie's mom told her to stay with the other kids. She promised, then raced outside.

Tony waited a few beats before turning back to Gayle. "A lot of people are heading outside. Let's meet some out there."

"Then we'll eat?"

Did the woman think about anything other than food? He nodded, trying to keep his demeanor calm. "Yes, then we'll get lunch."

"Great. Let's meet some people."

He took her hand and headed outside, eager to speak with Maisie again.

CONCERN

Zoey forced herself to eat a few bites of the nachos Alex had made from scratch and baked to perfection. Under any other circumstances, they would have looked delicious. Unfortunately, right now they made her stomach turn. But given how wonderful he was being, she didn't want to hurt his feelings.

He'd spent the whole night with her so she didn't have to be alone. Then he'd made her breakfast and lunch. Kept asking if she was okay. Did things for her she could do herself.

She loved him for it. Many guys weren't that doting even when the woman was carrying their own child. Zoey was carrying someone else's. Not that it was her fault, but still, she was.

"Is it good? Does the cheese need to be melted some more?" The kindness in his eyes nearly crushed her.

"No. These are the best." She forced a smile and took another bite. If she ate much more, she would end up with her face in the toilet. She probably would anyway, given the way things had been going.

Alex talked about everything from the academy to wedding plans to Ariana's science project. Zoey nodded along, nibbling on the same cheesy chip for twenty minutes while Alex ate the rest of the nachos.

He got up and kissed her forehead. "Why don't you lie down while I clean this up?"

She rose. "But you made it and breakfast. Let me."

Alex shook his head. "Nope. You rest, beautiful. I've got this."

Zoey tried to protest, but exhaustion squeezed her. "Once the second trimester hits, I'm going to start doing things for you."

"Sure thing." He kissed her again. "For now, sleep."

"How did I end up with the best fiancé in the world?"

"You didn't, because I did. Will the vacuum keep you awake if I run it?"

She stared at him. "You're going to vacuum my apartment?"

"Only if it won't disturb you."

Zoey put her hand on her stomach, her heart nearly shattering. "I really wish this was yours. It's such a cruel twist of fate."

A look of sadness crossed his face. "You know what would be worse?"

"What?"

"If the baby ends up being a half-brother or sister to Parker."

She gave him a double-take. "Parker? What are you talking about? What does he have to do with anything?"

"Don't tell anyone, but Nick said there's reason to believe Parker might not be his. Not naturally, at least."

Zoey covered her mouth. "Dave could be Parker's dad? You've got to be joking."

Alex shook his head. "Nick hasn't said anything to Parker, and he hasn't looked into the testing. He said it wouldn't change anything, that Parker is his son regardless."

Zoey closed her eyes and took in the news. "Could Corrine and Dave have ruined any more lives?"

Alex pulled her into a hug. "If you want, I'll raise the baby with you as if it were my own. Nobody ever has to know the truth."

Tears welled up in her eyes. "But everyone will know. I have to testify."

"Doesn't mean they'll automatically think it's his. You're engaged. Might even be married by the time the trial finally comes around. We can get married sooner if you want. I'm pretty sure if we're married, my name will automatically go on the birth certificate regardless of genetics."

She crumbled against him, and he tightened his grip around her, keeping her upright. "Maybe you should put more thought into this, Alex. Taking on someone else's kid as your own is huge."

He kissed the top of her head. "It's yours, and the only thing I want in this whole world is to be a family with you and Ariana. We can always have one of our own later. One that, like Ari, actually will be ours. Not that I'll treat this one any different. I swear."

Zoey blinked her tears away and sniffled. "While I love you so much for that, I want you to think about it some more. Maybe we can talk about it next weekend. Or in a month."

"There isn't anything to think about. I've already decided. It was never a question at all. We're in this together. You want to keep the baby and I want to keep you. That means this baby is ours as far as I'm concerned."

Tears stung her eyes. "Still, give it a week. For me?" She stepped back and stared into his eyes, blinking away the tears.

He gave a slight nod. "If that's what you'd like, but I won't change my mind."

"Thank you." Zoey gave him a quick kiss before heading into her room. Once there, she raced into the bathroom. She sat on the toilet, and that was when she saw it. The red on her underwear. Not just a little, either. It covered the fabric.

Shock ran through her. Was she losing the baby? Guilt stung at her for hoping she might be. After all, it was her child.

Zoey rose and saw the water in the bowl was red.

She was losing a *lot* of blood. Her chest tightened, and her mind raced. So much for taking a nap. She was going to have to take a trip to the hospital.

Heart thundering and tears threatening, she cleaned everything up and went to the kitchen to find Alex scrubbing the counter.

"Everything okay?" He dropped the sponge into the sink. "You're pale."

"I'm bleeding. A lot."

His face lost two shades of color. "What? Are you okay?"

She leaned against the wall. "A little dizzy."

"I'm taking you to the hospital. Sit down, and I'll grab whatever you need."

Zoey took some deep breaths, trying to ease the dizziness.

DOUBLE

Alex paced the little room as Zoey changed out of her clothes and filled a specimen cup in the bathroom.

What if something was really wrong? Had Dave given her a disease? Done something to permanently harm her? Or was it stress causing all the bleeding?

Hopefully it was the last one only. Until the day before, Zoey had been holding onto the news of the pregnancy all on her own—on top of dealing with everything else.

Alex knew firsthand how difficult it was to move on from an abduction. Both physically and mentally. Adding to that the strain of pregnancy, it was nothing short of a miracle that Zoey had held herself together for as long as she had.

The bathroom door opened. She stepped out, wearing a stiff-looking hospital gown.

He raced over to her. "Do you need anything?"

She grimaced. "For the bleeding to stop."

"I wish I could do something about that." He helped her over to the examination table and held her hand once she was settled. "Do you want me to find a blanket? It's kind of cold in here."

Zoey shook her head. "Just stay with me."

He kissed her forehead. "I won't leave your side."

She moaned and rested her free hand on her rounded belly.

"Does it hurt?"

"Just a little cramping."

"That doesn't sound good."

She closed her eyes and groaned.

Alex squeezed her hand and brushed some hair from her face. "I'm still here. I won't let anything bad happen to you."

Hopefully he could make good on that promise. He would do whatever he could to make that happen.

A few minutes later, a woman in a white lab coat came in, introducing herself as a doctor. She went over to the computer on a small desk and read over some notes and asked Zoey some questions.

Once she was done, she made more notes on the computer then turned back to Zoey. "I'm going to have an ultrasound machine brought in so we can take a look. How was the last one?"

Zoey's grip tightened around Alex's hand. "I haven't had one yet."

"This far along?" The doctor's eyes widened. A mixture of concern and judgment covered her expression.

Zoey bit her lip. "It... I... I'm not a bad mom!"

Alex glared at the doctor. "This pregnancy is the result of an assault. She's doing the best she can!"

The doctor's expression changed completely. "Why didn't you mention this before?"

"Does it matter?" Zoey's tone was defensive.

"It helps to have a full picture."

"Fine. I was abducted and raped. Now I'm pregnant. Does that explain my bleeding?"

Knock, knock.

A man and a woman entered with a rolling table full of computer equipment. It had to be the sonogram machine.

Alex clung to Zoey's hand while they prepared her.

As one of the technicians squeezed lubrication onto Zoey's stomach, the doctor's eyes widened. "Are you sure about how far along you are?"

Alex's stomach twisted. "Of course she is. Why?"

"Judging by the size of her belly, she should be further along."

"This isn't my first pregnancy." Zoey squeezed Alex's hand. "I'm showing faster. That's all."

Alex's mind raced as the technician's explained what was on the screen, though it was obvious. Even though the baby looked more like a bean than a person, it was clear which end was the head and which was the feet.

The doctor stepped closer. "Move it to the right."

The technician did.

"More." The doctor nudged the wand.

Alex's mouth dropped open. "Is that…?"

Zoey lifted her head off the pillow. "A second baby?"

"Two of them?" The room spun around Alex. Zoey was not only pregnant with one of Dave's babies, but two? Could this get any worse?

Alex sat in the chair, unable to process anything anyone said. He still held Zoey's hand.

How could this be happening? Wasn't it bad enough that they had one baby to deal with? Now two? Two!

His mind continued racing until he realized the technicians were leaving with the machine.

He couldn't get the image of the two babies from his mind.

The doctor was speaking. She sounded miles away.

Alex forced himself to concentrate. This was about Zoey, not him.

"…considered pregnancy options?"

"There's nothing to consider!" Zoey glared at the woman. "Just tell me why I'm bleeding so I can go home."

"Everything looks great. They both look as I would expect."

"Then why am I bleeding? Cramping?"

The doctor sat on the bed and gave Zoey a sympathetic glance. "Sometimes it happens, and we don't know why. It could be the strain of a twin pregnancy. I'm going to recommend you go on bed rest."

"What? Until when?"

"At least until the bleeding stops."

"I can't get up at all?"

"You can use the bathroom."

Zoey groaned, then turned to Alex. "Will you stay with me?"

"Yes, but I have academy all week."

"Right. I forgot. Maybe my mom can come over. That means I have to tell her about being pregnant."

"Or you could stay over at their house during the week. My parents can check on you during the day. Dad works at home."

"You two are together?" asked the doctor.

"Yeah." Zoey rubbed her temple. "Why?"

"Would you be interested in a paternity test? To find out for sure whose babies these are. Maybe set your mind at ease if they're actually yours." She glanced at Alex.

Alex gave her a double-take. "You can do that? While they're in the womb?"

"Yes. There is a slight chance of miscarriage, but it's very low. This procedure is common. It's how we check for Down's Syndrome."

Zoey turned to Alex, worry in her eyes.

Alex squeezed her hand and turned to the doctor. "Will it hurt Zoey?"

"Not at all. Nor the babies."

"Unless I miscarry." Zoey's hand tightened in Alex's.

"It's a very low likelihood."

She turned to Alex. "What do you think?"

"It's up to you."

The doctor leaned closer. "Any chance they're his? This could help you make the best decision."

"I'm not ending my pregnancy. Doesn't matter how the results come out."

"How long does it take to find out?" Alex asked.

"Depends on the lab. I can send it to the one that will process it faster. You could know in a few days."

Alex and Zoey exchanged a glance.

"It's up to you." Alex squeezed her hand again. "I'm here no matter what."

"Even with twins?"

Pressure squeezed from his temples to the back of his head. Their love was about sacrifice. She'd put up with a lot of his crap, forgiving him for far more than he deserved. Now it was his turn to step up to the plate and sacrifice for her. "Even with twins that aren't mine. All I want is you, and the babies are part of you."

Zoey turned to the doctor, her hands shaking in Alex's. "Let's do it."

LUNCH

The waiter brought over a basket of bread and set it in the middle of the table. "Are you ready to order?"

Maisie's dad turned to Tony and Gayle. "We are. Are you?"

Tony turned to Gayle. "Did you decide?"

"I did."

Tony smiled widely. "Looks like we're all set."

"Great." The waiter brought out a pad of paper and turned to him. "What are you having?"

Everyone ordered, then dug into the bread. They made small talk about the weather and the church service. Maisie worked hard on the various activities on her menu. She worked with such diligence, she hardly seemed to notice the adults. A rare quality in a child her age.

"Are you new to the area?" Maisie's mom asked. "I haven't seen you two around before."

Tony swallowed his bread and smiled. "Funny you should ask, Emily. No, but we don't live too far away. I am, however, considering this as a possible location."

Gayle gave him a double-take.

He ignored her. "Tell me, Emily. Is this a good area? Do you feel safe? Is it a good place for kids to grow up?"

Gayle shot him another look, which he ignored by focusing on Maisie's mother.

Emily nodded while sipping her soft drink. "It's great. We love it. It's the perfect community for raising a family."

"Wonderful." He reached for another piece of bread. "That's exactly what I was hoping to hear. And Ryan, is this a good place for many things like hunting and fishing?" He turned to Maisie's dad.

"I wouldn't know. There are some great tracks for racing, if you're into that. Bikes, cars, and even buses."

"Daddy likes to race his motorcycle." Maisie looked up from her coloring. "He wins a lot."

"Oh, I wouldn't say a lot." Ryan chuckled.

Tony asked about his bike and noticed Gayle and Emily exchanging a bored glance. Maisie, on the other hand, was happy about the discussion and piped in with praises for her dad's racing skills every so often.

The food came, and as they ate, the women changed the subject then dominated the conversation. Typical.

Tony had really missed out by not being born in a time where men were allowed to be men, and everyone else kept quiet unless spoken to.

He took a deep breath and tried to enjoy his salmon. It wouldn't be long before he would have Maisie to himself. Then he could raise her to be a proper young lady. The kind of girl that was sorely lacking in today's society.

It was a shame. A real shame.

But it wouldn't be long before Maisie trusted him enough to climb into his car for the present and the new balloon. Both were now in his trunk, since he was driving Gayle around today.

Later, he would try to bring Maisie to her new home. He had her bedroom all set up in the cabin. She would love it. Pink walls and bedding, posters of popular kids' cartoon characters, lots of dolls and books, and other knickknacks kids these days liked. Maisie would be so happy, she wouldn't even think about what she'd left behind.

They would have each other and would have no need for anyone else. No mean girls at school, no pushy mothers who posted everything online for the world to see.

If Emily wasn't careful, she could really get Maisie in trouble. Someone with nefarious motives could find and hurt the sweet child. They were lucky Tony was the one to find her before anyone else.

He would save her from becoming like every other woman in this wretched society of disrespectful women.

Speaking of which, Gayle and Emily were still yammering on about something insignificant. A new hair product or something. It was hard to keep up with the conversation, as it kept moving from one superficial topic to the next.

He turned back to Ryan and asked him something about motorcycles. As he'd hoped, Maisie joined in on the conversation, bragging about her dad's bike and racing skills.

The excitement in her eyes sent a warm chill down his spine. It was enough to make him wish he could take her right after lunch.

No, he had to play his cards right. He had to wait until she was ready to come willingly. And that would still take a little time.

When it did, nobody would give a second thought to a little girl climbing into a car on her own free will. And that was what he needed. To take her in such a way that was so normal, not a soul who saw would even recall it later.

Today was not his day. But soon.

Very soon.

PROGRESS

Genevieve pulled herself from the futon and trudged into the kitchen. Her body actually ached from reliving her nightmare in the woods. She could feel some of the long-gone gashes and bruises. There had been so many. She was lucky she hadn't walked away with any permanent damage—no lasting scars or any broken bones. Just sprains and cuts.

Tears threatened again, but she wasn't going to let them win. No, she was a tough officer of the law. Something that happened so long ago wasn't going to knock her down again.

It was bad enough that she'd broken down like that with Nick, but he'd proved to be the kind and caring man she'd known in her heart he was.

Now they'd both seen each other at their weakest. Her, reliving the night in the woods, and for him, his daughter missing. His tragedy had brought them together, then pushed them away. It looked like her mess would bring them together. Hopefully it wouldn't push them away from each other.

She certainly loved being in his arms. Hearing his soothing deep voice whispering words of comfort in her ears. She could definitely get used to that on a regular basis.

However, that would mean she needed to find a new precinct to work in before her time off ended. She wanted to kindle the sparks flying between the two of them far more than she wanted her current job. Given how understaffed most places in the area were, finding work nearby wouldn't be much of a challenge. Especially not if she got a glowing recommendation from her current captain.

She took a deep breath and went through the kitchen to see what there was for lunch. She wasn't too hungry after eating so much for breakfast, but Tinsley would be famished. The girl had been eating a lot lately—another fantastic change along with her speaking more.

Genevieve poked her head around the corner. Tinsley was still reading on the futon, sprawled across it.

"Hey, do you want me to warm up that casserole from last night?"

"Yeah, thanks." Tinsley didn't look up from her novel.

Genevieve tried to hide her excitement at Tinsley answering with more than a nod. If she brought attention to the speaking, she was afraid the girl might slip back into her shell. "Okay, it'll be a few minutes."

"Okay."

Genevieve headed back into the kitchen, beaming about the few words. Tinsley had spoken twice in a row. That was huge!

She bustled around the kitchen, warming the food up, glad to have some good things to think about. Between Nick and Tinsley, she was able to push the woods issue back as far into the past as it actually was.

A few minutes later, she set the two plates on the table. "Come and eat."

Tinsley slid her bookmark into place and joined Genevieve. "Smells good."

They exchanged a smile before digging in. Genevieve considered saying something else about it, but was hesitant to attempt an actual conversation.

When she was about halfway through her food, Tinsley looked at her. "Hanna's funny."

"What did she do?"

"She snuck up on the cat. It jumped this high." Tinsley held her hand about waist-high and giggled.

"That is funny." Genevieve forced herself to laugh as she covered her shock at Tinsley speaking two full sentences in a row. Would this turn into a new normal?

Tinsley giggled a little more before going back to her food.

Genevieve made a mental note to make sure Tinsley had more time with Hanna. Even though they had an age gap—Tinsley was closer to Ava's age—the two girls just connected more, probably because of everything Tinsley had been through. And besides how good their friendship was for Tinsley, it was also the perfect excuse to see more of Nick.

Her heart skipped a beat at the thought. Nobody was perfect, but he was close. Gorgeous and commanding of respect, yet tender and compassionate when he needed to be. What wasn't there to be enamored by?

"Help with dishes?" Tinsley's voice brought Genevieve back to the present.

It took her a moment to process what the girl had said. "You want to help me with the dishes?"

Tinsley nodded.

"I can't say no to that." She smiled and pushed back her seat. "Wash or dry?"

"Wash." Tinsley grinned.

They laughed and had fun cleaning up the mess in the kitchen, then Tinsley went back to her book, without a word, but smiling.

Genevieve was about to check for nearby police openings when the front door unlocked. She expected it to be her mom, but it was her dad, returning from who-knew-where. Probably fishing. Again.

"Where'd you go?" she asked.

He hung his coat on the rack. "Took your advice. Went to blow off some steam where people would see me. Lots of witnesses."

She arched a brow. "Really? Where?"

"To a park."

"A park?"

"Lots of kids and parents."

"Why a park?" She studied him, trying to make sense of it.

He shrugged. "I'm tired. Going to take a nap."

"Are you hungry? I can warm up that casserole. That's what Tinsley and I had."

"I just ate. Couldn't possibly have more."

"You ate? At the park?"

"No. I ate at a restaurant."

"You said you went to a park."

He shook his head. "What is this, the third degree? I went to a park and then a restaurant with my friend Bill. We walked around the track a few times, then decided to grab lunch. I'm stuffed and ready for a Sunday afternoon nap."

At least he hadn't gone fishing again. "Thank you for taking my advice."

He gave her a tired smile then put his hand on her shoulder. "I appreciate your concern. I really do."

Then he lumbered into the bedroom. A moment later, the shower started.

Genevieve stared at the closed door. Maybe he would be taken off the persons-of-interest list if he kept this up.

HURRY

Alex glanced around the now-empty grocery aisle and scanned the rows of feminine products in front of him. He was supposed to pick up pads for Zoey's bleeding.

Which of the many, many products were the pads? Everything had different names, and all he knew was he wasn't to get tampons.

Why were the lights so bright? Were they always so bright?

It was hard to think with so many choices. So many brands. So many colors.

He pulled out his phone and texted Zoey.

Alex: Which ones am I supposed to get?

Zoey: I don't care.

A couple of teen boys walked down the aisle and snickered at him.

Alex: Daytime or night?

Zoey: Doesn't matter.

Alex: Help me help you. Please. People are staring.

Zoey: Night.

At least that was something. He reached for a package but then wasn't sure if he should get that one or the one next to it.

Alex: Do you care about wings?
Zoey: No.
Alex: OK. Be home soon. Hope I get the right stuff.
Zoey: I'm sure it's fine.

"That's what she says now," he mumbled. Alex grabbed a black package with neon pink writing and shoved it under a hunting magazine next to the dinner he'd picked up at the deli. Alex wasn't into hunting, but his shopping basket needed a strong dose of masculinity thanks to the nighttime winged feminine pads.

He hurried toward the registers, but froze in place. "You have got to be kidding me."

Flynn again.

He was comparing two greeting cards.

Alex balled his fists. Having his friends send him texts wasn't enough?

He stormed toward the older man, acid churning in his gut. It would take all of his energy not to punch the weasel in the face.

If he did that, he would get carted off to jail. He couldn't afford that. Not when he was in the middle of the academy. Not when Zoey was lying in bed, waiting for him. For the pads. Bleeding with two babies inside of her.

Alex took a deep breath and texted Nick, telling him that Flynn was there in the grocery store. To prove his point, Alex snapped a picture of him.

But Flynn moved just as Alex snapped the picture, but all he got was the back of the jerk's head. He waited, but Flynn didn't turn back. Instead, he put one of the cards back and walked the other way.

The phone buzzed with a text.

Zoey: You almost here?
Alex: Just about.

He sent Nick the picture, even though it wasn't much. The back of a head.

If everyone at the station didn't already think he was crazy about the Flynn thing—the man was supposed to be on death row—he would call them and report the sighting. And if Zoey didn't need him right then, he'd confront the snake.

How was he getting away with it? Walking around free?

Anger pulsated through Alex as he made his way through the store to the registers. He barely kept his cool as he made small talk with the cashier, who thankfully made no mention of the pads.

Alex looked for Flynn as he made his way out of the store. He couldn't see him, but he knew he was there. Somewhere.

DECISIONS

Nick balanced the pizza boxes while the kids ran ahead and knocked on the condo door.

"We have dinner!" Hanna yelled as she knocked.

"There are neighbors," Nick reminded her. "They don't like yelling."

The door flung open, and Tinsley stood there. "Pizza!"

"Yeah!" Hanna grabbed her arm and jumped up and down. "We got your favorite!"

"Hawaiian."

Nick readjusted the boxes. "Yep. Can we come inside?"

Tinsley ran inside with Hanna. The other two followed, then finally Nick. He kicked the door closed.

Genevieve appeared around the corner. She wore a pale pink dress, and it was the perfect complement to her tanned skin and dark hair.

She took his breath away.

"Let me get those." She grabbed the pizza boxes from him before he could protest.

The kids had already gathered around the table.

"Where are your parents? I got enough pizza for everyone."

"You're so sweet." She set the boxes down and pulled out some plates from the cupboard. "They went out to visit some friends. I'm sure they appreciate the thought."

"Well, you can keep the leftovers. I'm sure there'll be plenty."

"No doubt."

His kids all talked over each other as they ate, and surprisingly, Tinsley even got a few words in. After devouring most of the pizza, the kids piled onto the futon and found a movie to stream.

Genevieve and Nick picked up the mess and headed out to the patio. His ears rang from the sudden silence.

Genevieve smiled at him. "Thanks for bringing the pizza over. Tinsley loves it when the kids come over. She's been talking so much more lately."

Nick smiled. "I'm glad. Seems like you two are good for each other."

Genevieve shrugged. "I really haven't done much."

"Haven't done much?" Nick gave her a double-take. "You've brought her in and been her advocate. It's no small feat going from living single to taking on a kid. Especially one with a past like hers."

Genevieve glanced inside. "I'm just glad I can help her. I was surprised she clung to me as she did, but I suppose we're kindred spirits."

Nick rubbed her shoulders. "You certainly are."

Genevieve pulled close to him and sighed. "We probably shouldn't do this while I'm still employed at the station."

Nick's heart sank. "Oh. Right."

She spun around, a fire in her eyes. "That's why I'm officially giving you my resignation. I quit, Captain. I already applied at the three closest precincts."

The corners of his mouth twitched. "You did?"

"Yes, sir. And now that it's official, I can do this." She pressed her soft lips on his and deepened the kiss immediately.

Nick's pulse raced. He kissed her back with pent up passion, but still keeping himself in control as the kids were just inside, not far out of view.

Genevieve pulled back and pressed her palm on his chest. She stared at him with an intensity in her eyes.

He wanted to take possession of her mouth, but he held back. Moving too fast before was what had ended up pushing them apart. He'd nearly lost her because of giving into his desires.

Nick studied her bright gray eyes, trying to believe this was actually happening. That if it weren't for the dead bodies in her parents' yard, he wouldn't even know where she was.

She pressed her other palm on his chest, and his breath caught.

If she kept looking at him like that, he wouldn't be able to keep himself from planting his lips on hers again. She obviously wanted this as much as he did—she'd already applied at different departments so they could be together.

He leaned closer.

His phone rang.

Disappointment washed through him. "Sorry. Might be the station."

She nodded.

He hated to ruin the moment, but he had to check it. And it was Anderson. "Fleshman here."

"Sorry to bother you, Captain."

"What is it?"

"I thought you should know they ID'd another body."

"That's good, but you're not going to call me each time, are you? There are going to be a lot of these rolling in over the next few days."

"I know, sir, but this one also has a connection to our person of interest."

Nick's stomach twisted. "What do you have?"

Genevieve watched him, her expression growing concerned. As it should've been, given the news Nick was about to hear.

"The two families were next door neighbors. The girl would've been about Officer Foster's age. Sir, she may have been friends with the victim. We need to find out if that's the case."

Nick swore and turned away from Genevieve. "What's her name?"

"Leigh Monaco. She was eleven when she was taken. How do you want to handle this? Do you want to ask the Fosters about this? Garcia and I can call them in."

"No. I'm not far from the condo. I'll talk with her."

They ended the call and Nick slowly turned back to Genevieve.

"It's not good news, is it?" Genevieve asked slowly.

He shook his head. "One of the victims was a neighbor of yours at the time. Same age as you."

Her eyes nearly popped out of her head. "What? Who was it?"

Nick took her hand. "Did you ever know a Leigh Monaco?"

"Leigh? She wasn't kidnapped. She went to live with her grandparents." Realization that she'd been told a lie spread across her face. "She never went with them, did she?"

He shook his head. "I'm sorry."

Genevieve's brows came together and her nostrils flared. "My best friend was killed, and my parents never told me the truth? Never gave me the chance to mourn? To grieve?"

Nick squeezed her hand, then pulled her close. "I'm really sorry. I'm sure they were just trying to protect you since you were so young."

"How dare they!" She shook against him.

He rubbed her back. "I think we need to prepare for the worst, Genevieve. It's possible your father may have been involved, and I need to get to the bottom of this. Or at least have my guys find out the truth. I may have to remove myself from this case, or we're going to have to stop seeing each other until this is solved."

She continued shaking. "Do what you have to do."

"Would you prefer I take myself off the case? I don't want to be the one to…" He let his voice trail off, not wanting to finish the sentence.

"Arrest my father," Genevieve said for him.

"Right."

"Do what you have to," she repeated.

Nick pulled out his phone and called Anderson back.

"Did you talk to her?" Anderson answered.

"Yes. Genevieve knew the vic but didn't know the girl had been taken. I need you and Garcia to question Walter. He's at a friend's house."

"I'll get on that right away."

"Thanks, Anderson." Nick ended the call and held Genevieve, who sobbed in his arms for the second time that day.

FLINCH

Zoey opened her eyes, not wanting to wake. She was on the couch, leaning against Alex, who was texting with a tense expression on his face.

"Are you okay?" Her voice came out scratchy. She cleared her throat.

He turned to her, his frown disappearing and his eyes filling with concern. "Did I wake you?"

She shook her head. "I think it was the TV."

"How are you feeling?" He set aside his phone.

"Who are you texting?" She craned her neck to see the screen.

"No one."

"You expect me to believe that? You have to be texting somebody."

Alex frowned. "You're right. I just didn't want you to worry."

"Worry? About what?" Had he heard something from the hospital? She almost didn't want to know. "Is everything okay?"

He took a deep breath. "I've been getting texts from someone who says Flynn wants to see me."

Zoey's heart skipped a beat. "Ariana's abductor? He wants to see you?"

He nodded. "Unfortunately."

"The man who almost killed her?" Rage pulsated through her body. "He's contacting you?"

"Not him directly. He's supposed to be in jail. That's where he wants me to visit him. I don't know what to think."

"You still think he's out?"

Alex's brows drew together. "He *is*. I've seen him."

"Someone who looks like him?"

"No! Not unless he has a twin nobody knows about—and that's ridiculous. It's him. I could never forget that face."

"It just doesn't make sense."

"Tell me about it. Believe me, I've questioned my own sanity over this more than once. I know how it looks." He took a deep breath. "But I don't want you worrying about this. I'm going to ignore him. Are you hungry? Thirsty?"

Her stomach lurched at the thought of food. "Just tired."

Alex kissed her cheek. "Why don't we get you ready for bed? I should get some sleep, too. I have to get up early to drive to the academy tomorrow. Unless you need me to stay. I will if you want me to."

She shook her head. "No, you need to go. I'll be fine. I have to work, anyway. I'm going to talk to my boss about working from home part of the week."

"Part of the week? You're on bedrest, Zo. You can't go in at all."

She frowned. "I might start to feel better in a few days. My bleeding seems to be lighter."

He shook his head. "No work. You heard the doctor—bed rest. Are you going to tell them about the pregnancy?"

"I'm going to have to, although they're bound to figure it out eventually whether I say anything or not. Can't hide it, especially not with twins."

"True." He looked deep in thought. "Do you want me with you when you tell your parents and Ariana?"

Pain pressed on her temples. "How are we going to explain this to Ariana? That these babies aren't yours? That I was violated and—?"

"We won't." Alex enveloped her into his embrace. "We're getting married and I'm raising them as if they were my own because they're yours. There's no reason for anyone to think they aren't mine."

"But I have to testify against him. What if they question the paternity then?"

"Why would they? You were engaged when he abducted you. There's no reason anyone would think you weren't already pregnant. He violated you, that's all anyone needs to know. We'll get married, then my name will be on the birth certificates."

"But what if people ask about Dave being the father? What do I say then?"

"Tell them that I'm the twins' dad. I'm going to raise them with you, so I *am* their dad. And besides, asking if he raped you is horrible. It's none of their business!"

"What if the twins ask questions later? We can't hide the truth from them if they suspect anything."

Alex cupped her chin. "I doubt they will. Even so, we have plenty of time to worry about that. At least twelve years. Maybe more. For now, let's just make sure you're taken care of. Who's going to watch you tomorrow?"

She pulled away. "I don't need a babysitter."

"You're not supposed to get out of bed."

"Then why am I on the couch?"

"Because you're resting. I'm going to carry you back to bed, remember?"

Annoyance ran through her. "I can walk."

"I know you *can*. That's not going to stop me from carrying you. Sure you don't want something to eat before going to bed?"

"Not unless you want me puking."

He shook his head. "No. Do you want me to see if the doctor can prescribe you something for the nausea? You need to eat something. Especially with two babies in there, taking their nutrition from you."

"I'm still eating. Just not a lot."

"Are you getting enough?"

"I think so. Especially since I'm not going to need any energy for walking around."

He frowned. "You say your bleeding has gotten better?"

"It's hard to tell, but I think so."

"Well, I'll take you so you can check." He scooped her up and carried her into the bathroom. "Let me know if you need anything."

She leaned against the counter and nodded.

Alex closed the door behind him.

Zoey took a deep breath and got herself ready for bed, trying to ignore the fatigue squeezing her.

"How are you doing in there?" Alex asked after a few minutes.

Part of her wanted to be annoyed with him, but she couldn't help loving him more for all of this. He certainly didn't have to stick around to help her raise *two* babies that weren't his. Especially since it basically killed their dream of having more kids together.

"Everything okay?" He sounded worried.

"Almost done. I'm fine."

She hurried as best she could, but found the longer she stood made her dizzy. Once done, she opened the door to find Alex two inches from her.

"How are you feeling? Did the bleeding stop? Do you need anything?"

She pressed a palm on the doorframe. "I just need to lie down. The bleeding has almost stopped. Almost."

He breathed a sigh of relief. "That's good news." Then he scooped her up again and carried her over to the bed and tucked her in. "How's that?"

She rested her head on the pillow. "Perfect. Thanks for everything. You don't know how much I appreciate it."

"I'm here for you, Zo. No matter what." He climbed on the bed and traced her jawline, gazing into her eyes.

Zoey swallowed, overcome by emotions.

Alex rested his hand on her shoulder and drew closer.

She flashed back to the woods. To Dave approaching her. Violating her.

She pulled back and gasped for air.

Alex jumped and let go. "What's the matter? Did I do something wrong?"

Zoey blinked a few times. It took her a moment to realize she was safe in her bed. That Alex was with her. He would never intentionally hurt her.

"Zo?" Worry filled his eyes.

"I'm sorry, Alex. I don't know what to say."

"Don't be sorry. Don't ever be sorry." He pulled her close and rubbed her back.

WISTFUL

Genevieve kissed Tinsley's forehead, then left the bedroom, leaving the door open just a crack.

Exhaustion swept through her, pressing on her temples and on every muscle in her body.

Light shone from underneath her parents' door, and she could hear hushed tones from inside the room. At least her dad had spent the whole evening with others and was now settling into bed for the night.

She wanted to ask him about the latest development—the one behind her aching fatigue. Leigh Monaco, who Genevieve had always believed had gone to live with her grandparents. She had been dead all this time. Dead!

Her dad wasn't going anywhere now. If he tried to sneak out early, Genevieve would wake and question him. She needed to hear the answers herself.

Why had they hidden the death from her? Because they thought she was too young to know the truth? Genevieve could accept that, but paired with the fact that her Dad also knew the father of the first victim and the fact that they were now living in their old house, it was too much to be a coincidence.

She stared at her parents' door, half wanting to knock and half wanting to climb onto the futon and let sleep take her away from everything. Instead, she crept into the bathroom. That would give her a few minutes to think about what she should do.

Except she already knew what she *should* do. She should confront him and get answers. With Tinsley asleep, there was no better time than the present.

Still, there was part of her that didn't want to face what could potentially be the truth. Was it possible her dad had been murdering girls since before Genevieve was born?

Her entire body went cold. Her hands shook.

Breathe. Focus. Think.

"You're a cop," she mumbled. "You can do this. This is what you do for a living."

But this was different. Way different.

Tears stung her eyes, and she caught sight of her reflection. Instead of a tough police officer, she saw the scared teenager who had barely escaped the nightmare in the woods. Terrified. Exhausted. Alone. Beaten.

She washed her face and avoided the mirror. It was too much —facing her past and her father all in one day. But it had to be done.

Her mind raced as she finished getting ready for bed. She would demand answers. He'd been claiming innocence the whole time, so he had to have reasonable explanations. She hoped.

What would she do if he didn't? Could she keep going if her worst fears turned out to be true?

A horrible thought struck her. What if her mom was involved? They had both hidden Leigh's death from her. Both told Genevieve that her best friend had moved to her grandparents' house. She'd been eleven. Old enough to handle the truth. It would've crushed her, sure, but she had deserved the truth.

Genevieve forced herself to look at her reflection. She stared into her eyes until she saw strength rather than weakness. No, strength *in* the weakness. Then she held onto that and marched out of the bathroom.

A door closed.

She looked around. The light under her parents' door was out. Everything was dark, except for the lamp next to the futon.

Genevieve tiptoed to her parents' door and turned the knob. She could see the silhouette of the bed—and only one person lying in it.

Her heart sank, and as she crept over, she saw exactly what she had known she would—her mom alone. Their bathroom was empty.

She explored the rest of the condo, still not finding him. Peeking outside revealed Dad's car was gone from where he'd parked it earlier.

It was time to face the facts. He looked guilty, so he probably was. There was no solid evidence, but it was only a matter of time. The truth would eventually come to light. Especially with the rate at which evidence was pointing to him, even if still only circumstantially.

Genevieve collapsed on the futon and shook.

Her dad had always been her hero. When she was a little girl, she'd seen him as perfect and strong. The man could do no wrong in her eyes. She was old enough to know nobody was infallible, but it gutted her to think she'd could have been so completely wrong about him.

Innocent until proven guilty.

Would that hold up? Was there any hope left that he could be innocent?

If only he would help them help him. She would do anything to help, but all he was doing was pushing her away. Making himself look guiltier and guiltier.

Why keep taking off? Alone, no less?

She pulled out her phone and sent him a quick text.

Genevieve: Where are you?

Dad: Went to check on the house.
Genevieve: It's a crime scene.
Dad: Still my house.
Genevieve: Why not take me?
Dad: Next time I will.
Genevieve: How does it look?
Dad: Fine. Still has yellow tape keeping us out.
Genevieve: Come back here. OK?
Dad: OK. Need anything from the store?
Genevieve: No. Just come home.
Dad: The condo isn't home.
Genevieve: You know what I mean.
Dad: Be there soon.

She frowned as she reread the conversation. Why would he go to the house at this hour? Was he really just checking on his property? Or was he going back to the scene of the crime?

Genevieve hated herself for doubting him, but what other option did he leave her?

She went over to her reading app and opened a book about a young vampire in denial of her destiny. It was the perfect escape from the real world while she waited for her dad to get home.

Except that after a few chapters, her eyes fell closed. And he still hadn't returned.

PATIENCE

"Would you put the phone down?" Gayle glared at Tony from behind her fashion magazine.

He kicked his feet up on the coffee table and tucked his phone into his pocket, careful not to let her see the screen with Maisie's photo.

She kept her magazine in front of her. "What's so interesting?"

"Just Twitter. Everyone's freaking out about the president's latest tweet."

Gayle yawned. "Boring. I thought we were going to watch a movie. Or we could take it to the bedroom."

He shook his head. "Not tonight."

"You're the most boring boyfriend I know of. I suppose you're going to go back to your place after the movie, too?"

"Yeah. What's wrong with that?"

"We could both save on rent if you moved in."

"You know how much I value my privacy."

"That can't last forever." Gayle stared him down.

"Why not?"

"Are you serious?" Her eyebrows drew together.

"I need space. Lots of it."

She groaned. "Is this relationship going anywhere? I seriously thought when you wanted me to come to church with you, we were scoping out wedding venues."

"No. Just checking the church. I liked it, didn't you?"

She sighed. "And what was up with inviting that family out for lunch? That was just weird. We don't even know them. And we don't have kids their age."

"Weird?" He sat up straight. "Why was it weird?"

"For real? It's not like we have anything in common with those people. I'm divorced with grown children and you're perpetually single."

"Right." He squirmed. "They just seemed like nice people. We need friends. People to hang out with. We can look for other friends, if you'd prefer."

"That would make more sense. Emily and Ryan are like half our age. We should find some people we have something in common with if we're going to spend time with anyone."

"Who do you want to be friends with, then?"

She shrugged. "I dunno. We can find some other couples closer to our age. There's gotta be a website for that sort of thing."

"Probably. Or we'll sit at a different part of the church next week."

Gayle didn't reply. They sat in silence for a few moments before she grabbed the remote and brought up a list of movies to stream. "What are you in the mood for? I was thinking a romantic comedy, but suddenly I'm not in the mood."

He held back an eye roll. "Whatever you want. I don't really care."

Gayle narrowed her eyes. "You're really frustrating, you know that?"

"Why? What did I do? I said you could pick."

She threw her hands in the air. "Never mind!"

"Fine. I won't." He turned back to his phone and checked

Emily's social media profile. She'd uploaded a picture of Maisie sleeping in bed while he'd been arguing with Gayle.

Maisie was a perfect little angel. She didn't talk back or make annoying demands. It would be so nice when it was just the two of them in his cabin.

Patience.

"Just go home!" A pillow hit him in the side of the head.

He turned to Gayle, lowering his phone. "What?"

"If you're going to ignore me, just leave. You're a terrible boyfriend. I don't know why I put up with you!"

Anger surged through him. Everyone wanted something from him. Nobody appreciated him. And nobody ever wanted to do anything *for* him. It was all about what he could do for them.

He glanced back at the screen in hope that the sweet image of Maisie could calm him down enough to have a rational conversation with Gayle.

Instead of Maisie, he saw Emily's latest status update. A picture of her legs propped up on a leather ottoman with her perfectly manicured hand holding a glass of wine.

That gave him an idea.

He stuffed his phone in his pocket. "We're both on edge. Why don't you pick out a movie, and I'll pour us some wine? How does that sound?"

Gayle's expression softened. "Really?"

He imagined Maisie sleeping so peacefully and managed a genuine smile. "Yes, really. I'll pop some popcorn, as well."

"Wow. Okay. Any movie I want?"

"Yes. Even the one about the rock star and the puppy I said I'd never watch."

Her eyes lit up. "I'm not sure what just happened, but I'll take it."

He gave her a quick kiss, then headed for the kitchen. As the popcorn popped, he pulled out his phone and scrolled through

Emily's profile, skipping each narcissistic image of Emily and stopping at each picture of Maisie.

There was a particular sweetness about her that was lacking in so many kids her age these days. She was a rare little bird, and she deserved so much better than her parents were giving her.

He couldn't wait to give it all to her. It was just a matter of finding the right opportunity. He'd already established trust. Familiarity. Friendship.

They'd talked at school, at home, at her party, at church, and at lunch with her parents. Maisie knew he had a present for her because she was special. She'd accepted the balloon.

The next step was the big one. Getting her into the car for her gift. Once that happened, he would take her to the cabin and show Maisie her new pink bedroom.

A warm thrill ran through him. They could be together forever, and he could teach her to stay sweet and innocent, unlike every other girl on the planet who lost those qualities in the teenage years. Often earlier, nowadays.

The microwave beeped. He took out the bag and dumped it into a large bowl, barely paying attention. His mind was stuck on being in the cabin with Maisie.

He balanced the wine glasses and popcorn bowl as he walked into Gayle's living room.

She beamed when he came into the living room. "You're in such a good mood. Did you sneak some wine already?"

"Not yet." He handed her the bowl and set the glasses on the coffee table.

Once he settled onto the couch, she started the movie. It was the rock star one. After all he'd just done for her, she'd still picked the one she knew he didn't want to watch.

Typical.

All the more reason to appreciate Maisie. Soon, he wouldn't have to deal with Gayle at all.

ADVISE

Nick leaned against the wall behind him and took a deep breath. Walter sat at the table on the other side of the two-way mirror. He stared at the cup of coffee Nick had given him, but didn't do anything else.

Walter looked tired, maybe bored, but otherwise didn't give off any guilty vibes. He wasn't talking to himself, pacing, muttering, or gesturing toward the mirror as many of the guilty people did.

Garcia came in and glanced over at the mirror. "How do you want to handle this, Captain?"

"I'm going to question him alone."

Garcia nodded. "Going for the friendly approach?"

"Yeah. If that doesn't work, I'll have you or Anderson question him. Press him for details. We'll see what works for him."

"Sounds good. I'll stay here."

Nick gave a quick nod, tossed his empty foam cup into the trash, then headed into the interrogation room. "Sorry that took so long. I'm up to my ears in paperwork."

"It's no problem." Walter barely glanced up at him.

"You getting enough rest?" Nick sat across from him and rested his chin in his palm.

"Yeah. Appreciate you letting us stay in your condo."

"Glad to help. Your daughter is an important part of our force."

Nick waited for Walter to say something.

He didn't.

"Where were you last night?" Nick asked.

"Went with my wife to play board games with some friends. Three people to vouch for me."

"That's good. What about after that?"

"Went home."

"Didn't go anywhere after that?"

Walter's mouth formed a straight line. "You talked to Genevieve?"

Nick nodded. He didn't dare say more. Not after sneaking in a few mind-melting kisses in the middle school parking lot after dropping off the kids at school. He hadn't yet processed her resignation, so she was still technically part of their force.

Walter cleared his throat. "Like I told her, I was checking on the house."

"Did you go in?"

"I'm not stupid." He sat up straight. "Drove up, got out, and looked around—without going near the police tape."

"What were you looking for?" Nick leaned forward.

"Just making sure everything was okay."

"What wouldn't be okay?"

Walter cleared his throat again. "Just making sure it was locked up tight. That nobody was messing with it. That's all. It's my home, after all."

"Makes sense."

"Do you know when we'll be able to go back? As much as I appreciate your hospitality, I'm sure we'd both like it if I could move my family back into the house. You can rent your condo out, and I can settle my family back where we belong."

"I understand. You'll be the first to know when you're clear to return."

"Thanks." Walter played with the coffee cup.

"What do you know about Leigh Monaco?"

He glanced up, his eyes wide. "Don't tell me she has something to do with this?"

"What do you know about Leigh Monaco?" Nick repeated.

Walter swore. "The girl went missing years ago. She was about the same age as Genevieve."

"And she was your next-door neighbor?"

Walter nodded, his expression tense.

"What was that like?"

"What do you mean?" Walter's lips formed a straight line. "She went missing. Nobody ever found her—although since you're asking about her, I have a pretty good guess where she ended up. My yard."

"So, you don't know anything about Leigh?"

"No! Why would I? Do I need a lawyer?"

Nick took a deep breath. "Speaking as a friend, you might want to get one. I believe you, Walter. I really do. But things are looking worse for you. Not everyone here is going to be so quick to accept your story."

Walter's face reddened. "I didn't do anything! It wasn't me! I don't know why I'm connected to two of the girls. There are others. I have nothing to do with any of the rest of them. That has to count for something, doesn't it?"

"Like I said, I believe you. There were a lot of girls dug up. It only makes sense that you'd have some connection to a couple. There are so many of them. Any one of us could've known one or two of them. We just have to wait for the rest to be identified."

Walter pulled on his hair. "I'm innocent, Captain. I swear. You believe me, right? I'm telling the truth."

Nick nodded. "That's why I think you should seek legal counsel. I don't want to see you say anything that could harm your case. Do you have an attorney, or do you want me to look into that for you?"

Walter shook his head, tears shining in his eyes. "Can I call my wife?"

"Of course. You're not under arrest. And even if you were, you'd be allowed a phone call. You have your phone?"

Walter nodded and swallowed.

"I'll give you privacy." Nick gave him a sympathetic glance before leaving the room to rejoin Garcia.

"What do you think?" Garcia glanced over at the window, where Walter was now speaking on the phone.

"He doesn't show any of the typical signs of guilt."

Garcia nodded. "I noticed that, as well. He had legit tears after you left."

The door burst open. Anderson came in, his eyes wide. "Two more bodies have been identified!"

"Please tell me they aren't related to Walter," Nick muttered.

Anderson shook his head. "Not that I'm aware."

Nick glanced over at Walter, who was still on the phone. "Let's hope the new information clears him."

Garcia frowned. "But then we're left without any other real persons of interest."

"There's a killer out there. We need to find *him*."

SPILL

Alex finished his energy drink and stared at the intersection. If he went left, he would go to Zoey's apartment. If he went right, he would end up at the station. He hadn't spoken with his best friend in what felt like forever. Nick would probably still be there.

He turned right. Macy had been spending the last two days with Zoey, which allowed Alex to spend the previous night at the dorms. It hadn't been as restful as he'd hoped, but what did he expect from dorms? It had saved him the stress of driving over a hundred miles round trip for the day and given him some time to think.

Now he wanted to talk to his best friend. Nick was probably busy with the case that was all over the news, but hopefully he could spare a few minutes.

Alex pulled into the main parking lot and hurried inside. He waved to the receptionist and let himself in with his keycard since he technically worked there as a cadet.

"Hey, Alex." Deputy Mackey looked up from her desk. "How's the academy treating you?"

Alex yawned before he could offer a response.

She laughed. "I know how that goes. How much longer?"

"A couple months."

"It'll be done before you know it." She smiled at him before turning back to her computer.

"Is the captain still in?"

"Yeah. I think he's getting ready to head out."

"Perfect. Thanks." Alex raced for Nick's office and knocked. He could see Nick flipping through files.

He looked up and waved Alex in.

"I didn't expect to see you." Nick seemed genuinely happy to see him.

Alex yawned again as he stepped in and closed the door behind him. "It feels like forever. How's that big case going?"

"It's a massive headache."

Alex arched a brow. "More than usual?"

"The property is Genevieve's parents'. She and Tinsley were the ones to find the first two bodies."

"What? Are you serious?"

"Unfortunately." Nick gestured for him to sit on the other side of his desk.

"How are…" Alex contemplated his wording. "…things going with her?"

A smile crossed the captain's face. "Better. She's applying at other precincts."

"Does that mean…?" Alex let the rest of the question hang in the air between them.

Nick nodded. "Once she's hired somewhere else and this case settles, we'll be in the clear."

"Nice." Alex held up his hand to give him a high-five.

The captain gave him a funny look, but didn't leave him hanging. He hit Alex's palm. "It's definitely good news, although there are complications."

"Like what?"

Nick set the files aside. "Her dad is a person of interest."

"Why?"

"Circumstantial evidence. A lot of it."

Alex scratched his head. "Do you think he's guilty?"

Nick shook his head. "No. He just happens to be loosely connected with some of the victims—and living where they were all buried."

"That's crazy. Who else are you looking at?"

"Plenty of people have called with tips, but nothing has panned out yet. It's a lot to sort through, and a lot of families need to be notified about the remains."

"I can help once I'm done with the academy."

"Hopefully we'll have our guy by then."

"Or at least have Genevieve's dad cleared." Alex stifled a yawn. "I can't wait to be done. These long days and the commute are a killer."

"You don't have to come home during the week, you know. That's why we're paying for you to stay in the dorms."

"I know, and I am using them some of the time. But Ariana is used to seeing me all week and Zoey—" He stopped himself before saying more.

Nick tilted his head, obviously knowing that something was up. "What's going on with Zoey?"

Alex's stomach tightened. "I really shouldn't say."

"Is everything okay?" Concern darkened Nick's expression.

"You're going to find out eventually, but don't say anything to anyone else for now."

Nick nodded. "What is it?"

Alex spilled everything, relief flooding him for getting it off his chest. Not only that, but his friend would know what to say.

Nick's brows ruffled and his mouth formed a straight line as Alex told the story. "I'm glad that man is already behind bars. I can't believe Corrine brought him into our lives."

Alex nodded. "Makes me wish I could dish out some vigilante justice."

"You really shouldn't say things like that here."

"Doesn't change how I feel."

"As long as it doesn't lead to action."

"It won't. Don't worry. My days of pulling stupid stunts are over. The academy is turning me into a changed man."

"It has a way of doing that." Nick drew in a deep breath. "When do you find out the paternity results?"

"Today or tomorrow, depending on how backed up the lab is. The doctor seemed sure it would be tomorrow most likely."

"Why are you here, then?"

Alex raked his fingers through his hair. "I don't want to get there and hear that she's carrying…" He struggled to get the words out. "That she's carrying Dave's children. For now, I can pretend they're mine."

Nick frowned. "I get that. I do."

Alex wanted to ask about Parker, if Nick was going to get his paternity tested. But he knew all too well how much a question like that could feel like a punch to the throat.

They sat in silence, both pondering that they could be raising a psychopath's children.

LISTEN

Genevieve set the card down. "I win. We're tied, two to two. One more for the win?"

Eyes shining, Tinsley nodded. She gathered up the Uno cards and shuffled half the large deck before moving to the other half.

Genevieve watched, amazed at how much progress Tinsley had made in such a short time. More in the last week than in the months beforehand. The girl was spending more time playing games with others than hiding behind her books. Genevieve's mom had taught her to play Bridge, and Tinsley had picked up on it and become addicted. It kept both of them busy while Tinsley wasn't in school or doing homework.

"You first."

Tinsley's voice brought Genevieve back to the moment. The game was already set up. She picked up her cards and sorted them.

"Ready to lose?" Genevieve teased.

Tinsley shook her head. "Go ahead and try."

They laughed as the game grew more intense and each one tried to keep the other from winning.

In the end, Tinsley won, leaving Genevieve with two cards.

"Did you let me win?"

Genevieve showed her the one red and one blue card. "Nothing I could've done if I'd wanted to. You won fair and square."

Tinsley beamed.

"Good job, kiddo. Want to help me with dinner?"

"Yeah." She gathered the cards and put them in the box.

Genevieve put on some music, and they made a big batch of spaghetti. It would be easy to reheat for her parents. They weren't likely to be back soon—if at all.

The house had finally been returned to them, but it was a mess from the police inspections. Genevieve had offered to help clean it up, but they hadn't wanted Tinsley to see it in such disarray.

That was fine with Genevieve. She had every intention of helping them the next day while Tinsley was in school. And she kind of liked having the condo for just the two of them.

After eating, Tinsley sat at the table with her homework while Genevieve cleaned up dinner. She sat, and exhaustion squeezed her. For being on sabbatical, she sure wasn't getting much rest.

She pulled out her phone and checked emails and social media, waiting for Tinsley to ask for help.

"Done."

Genevieve glanced up at Tinsley, who smiled.

"Already?" She slid her phone back into her pocket.

"Yep." The girl beamed.

"I'm impressed."

"Time for another game?"

Genevieve didn't want to think, much less play another game. "Watch a quick show before bed?"

Tinsley frowned. "I guess."

"Sorry, kiddo. I'm wiped out."

"It's okay. Go for a walk?"

Genevieve's aching muscles protested, but going for a walk sounded better than needing to think. "Sure."

Tinsley grinned.

They made their way outside and followed a bike trail down the hill behind the condos. It led to some thick trees—not quite woods, but enough for Genevieve to stop in her tracks.

Tinsley stopped beside her. "You don't like the woods, either."

Genevieve shook her head, trying to ignore her thundering heart. "No, I really don't."

"Bad things happen in there." Tinsley frowned.

"That they do." Genevieve put an arm around her. "We've both seen it."

"My mom wanted to kill Alex."

Genevieve flinched. She'd known Tinsley's mom had been responsible for the abductions and murders of police cadets and officers, but she'd never heard the girl speak of it. "You helped Alex, though."

Tinsley nodded. "I didn't want to hurt any of the men."

Genevieve's heart shattered for Tinsley. "Of course you didn't."

"Why did she like hurting them?" Tinsley stared at her with wide eyes.

That was a loaded question if she ever heard one. "I think she thought it was helping your dad."

"A policeman killed him when he robbed that bank."

Genevieve nodded.

"He shouldn't have done that."

She shook her head.

"Was my dad a bad guy?"

Tears stung Genevieve's eyes. Tinsley shouldn't have to worry about all this stuff. "I think he made some bad choices. He probably thought it was the best he could do. I know he loved you."

Tinsley nodded. "They would both be in jail if they were still alive, right?"

There was no denying that. Genevieve nodded. "They would."

"Am I bad?"

"No! No, you're not. You're a wonderful girl, and I have no doubt you'll make great decisions."

"But my parents…"

"Were their own people. They made their choices, and you'll make your own. Plenty of people go on to live their lives drastically different from their families."

"You're my family now?"

Genevieve's throat nearly closed. She pulled Tinsley into a hug to give herself a moment to recover. "Yes, I'm your family. I'm not going anywhere."

Tinsley wrapped her arms around Genevieve. "I hope you'll adopt me."

Everything spun around her. "I'd love to. I can look into making that happen, if you'd like."

Tinsley squeezed her harder.

Hopefully, that was something she could make happen.

ALMOST

Maisie went down the sidewalk, her toy Hummer bumping over sticks and rocks.

Tony stayed behind the car, watching her dad. Ryan continued working on the motorcycle, but never really went out of sight. He turned his back several times, but only momentarily.

Maisie turned around in a neighbor's yard and came back toward the house.

Tony's heart raced. He needed to get Maisie into his car. To the cabin. He wasn't sure how much longer he could wait.

His patience was starting to wear thin.

It was already Tuesday night. He'd been working on this since Friday. Friday!

Her school was impossible. He'd tried to get her to come with him, but those teachers had their eye on everything.

This was really his only chance. When she barreled up and down the sidewalk while her parents were distracted. Church might work, since her parents let her play outside with the other kids while they talked inside. But again, there were a lot of watchful eyes.

It was almost enough for him to consider finding a new kid.

Almost.

He was convinced Maisie was the one. With each kid he'd taken, it was always his hope that she would be the one he could let live. The one he could train to stay sweet and innocent. The one who wouldn't be tainted and become like every other woman out there.

Then he wouldn't have to worry about Gayle or anyone else. He could go to work every day, then return home to Maisie. It would be the perfect life. Assuming she was the one.

She had to be. This had been going on for years. Decades. He was getting older. Tired. Losing his edge. As much as he hated to admit it, he couldn't keep this up forever.

He glanced over at Ryan. Maisie's dad had his back to the driveway again, and he was hunched over the bike.

Perfect.

It was time.

Tony looked around to make sure no one else was in the area. He couldn't see anyone.

Maisie was now headed back down the other way. Toward his car.

His heart raced as he crossed the street and headed for the sedan.

"Hi, Tony!" Maisie waved.

He waved back and glanced over at Ryan, who didn't look up from his project.

Tony headed for his car and opened the trunk, pretending he had no interest in Maisie. He listened to the toy motor as it went a little farther down, then headed back his way.

"Whatcha doing?" Maisie stopped the Hummer.

He glanced over, feigning a surprised look. "Oh, I forgot you were here. I still have your birthday present. How did you like the balloon?"

She smiled widely. "I still have it. It doesn't float, though."

"No?" He frowned. "We'll have to fix that, won't we? I can get you another one."

"Really?"

"Yeah. Do you want to come with me? We could be back before your dad is done with his bike."

Maisie glanced toward the house. "I dunno…"

"Your parents know me. We went out for lunch, remember?"

She stuck a finger in her mouth and looked deep in thought. "Well, yeah. But I'm just supposed to stay here. On the sidewalk."

He nodded. "We wouldn't want you to break the rules."

Maisie shook her head.

"I still have your present, like I said. It's in the backseat. Maybe you could open it. It's been so long since your birthday. I've really been wanting you to open it."

She glanced into the backseat. "I like the wrapping."

"I picked it out just for you."

Maisie kept her attention on the gift inside.

"You can open it now if you want. I just know you're going to love it."

She glanced back and forth between the present and him. "What is it?"

He tilted his head. "I can't tell you that. It's a surprise. Come on. What do you say?"

Maisie bit her lower lip. "I guess my parents would say it's okay."

"Of course they would." He slammed the trunk. "They know me. And they'd want you to be happy, right? Opening a present would make you happy."

She nodded, clearly following the logic.

His pulse pounded through his body, making his breath hitch. He managed to find his voice. "Let's do this."

"Yeah."

He squeezed between her and the car, his skin on fire.

It was happening. This was actually about to happen.

The handle felt icy on his fingertips as he pulled. The door opened, releasing the vanilla aroma from the air freshener.

Maisie's eyes widened as she stared at the present.

He waved her in. "It's all yours."

She hesitated.

A string of profanities raced through his mind. He kept the smile on his face though. "All you have to do is open it. Then it's yours."

"Um…" She twisted a strand of hair.

"Maisie!" Ryan called. "Where are you? Time to come in!"

"I gotta go. Sorry!" She punched the gas pedal and raced the little Hummer toward her house.

Tony swore under his breath and slammed the car door shut.

He would get her the next day, one way or another.

His patience was officially extinguished.

RESULTS

Zoey stared out her window, bored of streaming shows and checking social media. More than anything, she wanted to go back to work. She couldn't even work online, as her boss had given her the week off, paid. If Zoey couldn't make it in the next week, then she would be allowed to work remotely.

Given that her bleeding still hadn't fully stopped, that was looking like it would be the way things played out.

Knock, knock!

Probably Macy. She'd been stopping by each day with baby Caden. They'd even spent the night when Alex had stayed at the dorm.

"Come in!" Zoey called.

The front door clicked as Macy fiddled with the keys and let herself in. "I come bearing food."

"You're a lifesaver! I hope it isn't chicken."

"Nope. That made me nauseous, too." Macy came into the bedroom, set the baby car seat by the door, then handed a fast food bag to Zoey. "Still craving tacos?"

"You know it." She reached into the bag and pulled out the first item she found. Zoey dug in, ravenous and glad her appetite was finally returning.

Macy's eyes widened. "Have you eaten anything since I was here yesterday?"

Zoey nodded, then swallowed her mouthful of food. "Alex made me eggs and toast this morning."

"Good." Macy reached into the bag and pulled out a burrito. "How are you feeling?"

"Tired of resting."

"I'll trade you." She yawned. "Caden was up half the night."

Zoey patted the other side of the bed. "Feel free to sleep."

"But I'm here to take care of you."

"And you just brought me food. I couldn't ask for more right now. Sleep. I'm sure I can find something to watch or read."

"Are you sure?" Macy glanced at the bed, a longing in her eyes.

"Totally."

"You don't have to say that twice." She tossed her wrapper in the trash and climbed under the covers.

"Kind of reminds me of the sleepovers we used to have."

Macy smiled. "Yeah. Except that we had a lot less to worry about back then."

"Isn't that the truth?" Zoey sighed. "Want to tell scary stories?"

Macy laughed. "I never was any good at those."

"No, you really weren't."

Macy shoved her. "Hey!"

"What can I say? When you're right, you're right."

They teased each other for a few minutes before Macy's eyes closed and she let out a little snore.

Zoey flipped through the streaming choices, bored out of her mind. She'd already watched everything she had any interest in. She finally settled on rewatching *Supernatural,* starting at the beginning.

By the time the third episode began, her bladder was screaming at her. Both Macy and Caden were still sleeping. She climbed out of bed and fixed the blankets around the baby before heading into the bathroom.

She brought her phone in to send Alex a quick text. He liked reading what she had to say on his breaks. But before she had a chance to open their texting conversation, her phone rang.

It was the doctor's office.

Zoey's heart raced and she stared at the screen. She answered it just before it went to voicemail. "H-hello?"

"Is this Zoey Carter?"

She took a deep breath. "Yes."

"Hi, Zoey. This is Nurse Chu from Dr. Ross's office. Your test results are in. The doctor said she would prefer you to come to the office for them, but since you're on bed rest I can give them to you over the phone. It's up to you."

"Why does she want me to come in?"

"The results are complicated. You're likely to have questions. She's available to speak with you over the phone if you'd like."

"Complicated?" Zoey's mind raced. "How can paternity results be complicated?"

"Would you like the results over the phone?"

"Yes, please." It took all of her energy not to snap at the woman.

"The babies have different fathers."

The bathroom closed in around her. "What?"

"Yes, ma'am. It doesn't happen often, but it does happen. The babies aren't identical. Each baby came from a separate egg, and they were fertilized by different men's sperm."

Zoey struggled to find her voice. "But that's not possible. It was days apart. I was kidnapped. It felt like forever. It was days. I know that much. You have to be wrong."

"Kidnapped? I'm so sorry." The nurse cleared her throat. "It's still possible. Sometimes when this happens, a woman will release the eggs separately. Close, but separately."

"Can stress cause it?"

"I really don't know. It could be possible. Maybe. You'd have to ask Dr. Ross."

Zoey swallowed. "Can I find out which one was fathered by who?"

"Baby A was fathered by the man who provided the sample when you were at the hospital."

"Oh." The good news was that one of them was Alex's finally hit her. They weren't both Dave's.

"Would you like to speak with Dr. Ross? She'll be able to answer your questions more fully than I can."

"Maybe." Zoey's mind spun out of control.

"I can have her call you. Or would you prefer to call with specific questions?"

"Um, I'm not sure."

"How about I have her call you at the end of the day if we haven't heard back from you?"

"Okay. Thank you."

They ended the call, and Zoey stumbled back into her bedroom.

The twins had different fathers. One of the babies belonged to Alex. Baby A. That was fitting.

She was still carrying the child of a psychopath. The other baby was Dave's. Not that he would ever get out of prison to fight for custody.

Not that he would ever find out about this, period.

Or would he? Would it come up in the court case?

Zoey climbed into bed, her breaths shallow. Her mind spinning, racing.

At least there was a shred of good news. She would take anything she could get at this point. Now she needed to wait until Alex stopped by after the academy to tell him the news.

Hopefully, he'd see it as good news.

Then there was the matter of telling their families about the pregnancy. Would they keep Dave's involvement a secret? Let everyone think both belonged to Alex? Legally, they would both be his. She would put his name on both certificates.

But it might come into question later. They might all find out when she had to testify. The whole world would know then.

SHOCK

Alex parked next to Zoey's car and yawned. It had been an especially brutal day at the academy. If Zoey hadn't been on bedrest, he would've gone to the dorm and slept until the next morning. But he couldn't do that to her, so he'd driven the fifty-plus miles, drinking mochas and energy drinks to stay awake.

Now he needed to keep from falling asleep to take care of her. With any luck, she'd just want to sleep like she had the evening before.

He headed to her apartment, saying hi to some other residents on the way. As he pulled out the key to Zoey's, his phone buzzed with a text.

Groaning, he checked it.

An unknown number. Just what he needed. More of that garbage.

He clicked to read the text.

Unknown: He still wants to see you.

"I'm not playing today." Alex shoved his phone into his pocket and stuck the key into the deadbolt.

His phone buzzed again.

Unknown: Don't ignore me.

Dots danced. Another text came in.

Unknown: Answer me before your booty call.

A chill ran down Alex's spine. Was he being watched? He looked around but didn't see anyone.

The phone buzzed again.

Unknown: Flynn wants you to visit him.

Alex: In prison?

Unknown: Where else?

Alex: A grocery store? My daughter's school?

Unknown: He can't. Gotta be Walla Walla.

Alex's blood boiled. Like he had the time or energy to drive to Walla Walla to go to the penitentiary anytime soon. Or like he wanted to see Flynn. But he didn't have another option from the looks of it. Not that he'd give in easily.

Alex: Tell him to find me.

Unknown: Can't.

Fury tore through him. He wanted to punch a hole in something. Like Flynn's face.

Instead, he turned the deadbolt and put the key into the knob.

His phone buzzed again.

He swore, but ignored it.

It buzzed again, then again.

Alex checked the texts, growing even angrier when he saw the new ones.

Unknown: Don't ignore him.

Unknown: Or me.

Unknown: Answer me before your booty call.

Alex spun around and studied the area. After not seeing anyone, he waved around a one-finger salute in case the texter was watching him.

His phone buzzed like crazy.

Unknown: We need a date.

Unknown: Now.

Unknown: Before you step inside.

Unknown: You'll regret ignoring us.

Unknown: Alex Mercer.

Alex wanted to hunt the jerk down and beat him to a pulp.

Zoey called him from inside the apartment.

Alex swore under his breath, then sent a final text.

Alex: Saturday. Now leave me alone.

Unknown: Perfect. Better show up.

Alex shoved the phone back into his pocket and went inside. He took a deep breath, then another and another. If another text came in, he was going to lose it.

Luckily, all was quiet.

"Alex?" Zoey called from her room.

He did his best to push aside his anger. "It's me. Do you need anything?"

"Some juice."

"Coming right up." He kicked off his shoes, washed his hands, then poured her some orange juice.

Zoey sat up and smiled when he entered her room. "Thank you."

"Of course." Alex handed the glass to her and kissed her forehead as she gulped it down. He focused on her, trying to calm himself.

She handed him the empty glass. "Is there anything to eat out there? I obviously haven't been shopping."

"I'll check. Either way, you'll have food. We can order online, and I'll pick it up or see if we can find delivery."

"Are you sure?"

"Why wouldn't I be?"

She frowned.

He sat and brushed his fingers across her jawline. "Are you okay?"

"I'm sick of being in bed…" Her voice trailed off like she had more to say.

Then he remembered she was supposed to get the paternity

results that day. Maybe that was what was bothering her—confirmation that she was carrying Dave's babies.

It certainly made Alex sick to his stomach.

"Did you hear from the doctor?" He took her hand in his.

Zoey drew in a deep breath and stared at something behind Alex.

He kissed her cheek. "Do you want to talk about it?"

She met his gaze. "One of them is yours."

It took him a moment to comprehend her words. "*One* of them?"

"Apparently, it happens. Two eggs, two set of sperm. Baby A is yours."

Alex thought back to the days leading up to Zoey's abduction. He thought he'd heard somewhere that sperm could hang around for a few days, maybe even a week. He couldn't remember for sure.

"It's a shock, I know."

He nodded. "How are you feeling about all of this?"

"I'm glad one of them is yours. I wish they both were."

Alex kissed her temple. "Like I said, I'm not going anywhere. So even if they were both his, that wouldn't change anything. We're still a family—you, me, Ari, and the babies. Both of them."

Tears shone in her eyes. "You don't know how much that means to me."

A lump formed in his throat. "Don't do this." He cleared his throat. "Don't make me cry. It's hard enough on me knowing what happened to you."

She threw her arms around him and squeezed. "I really don't know what I'd do without you."

Tears stung his eyes. "I said, don't."

"I can't help it. You're better than I deserve."

He sat back and stared her in the eyes. "Don't say that. Don't ever say that. I'm lucky to have *you*. I've made more stupid decisions than anyone I know. Why you chose me over Golden Boy, I'll never know, but I'll be forever grateful."

Zoey sniffled. "We're meant to be together, Alex. Things keep trying to tear us apart, but somehow, they never do. At least, not for long."

"You're right. Keep that in mind, because I'm not going anywhere. Those years without you in my life were the worst I've ever experienced. You're not going to get rid of me easily. In fact, I dare you to try."

She smiled and wiped an eye. "I'm glad to hear that, because I'm not letting you go without a fight. That's a mistake I'll only make once."

Alex pressed his mouth on her soft, sweet lips and kissed her deeply. He didn't know how he'd ended up so lucky, but he was beyond grateful. The fact that one of the twins was his was a sign from above that they were indeed meant for each other.

He wasn't going to mess it up this time.

LAMENT

Tony paced around the fountain, muttering under his breath. Maisie and her mom had been shopping in the mall for hours—hours!—and the annoying woman hadn't taken her eyes off the girl for a single moment. She'd even taken her into the same bathroom stall.

Normally, he would have given up by now. Five solid days of frustration. Sure, sometimes it took longer to get a kid, but time was not on his side. Not this time. He wasn't getting any younger. Neither was Maisie.

And aside from that, every night on the news, they announced more of his treasures having been identified. Some nights, they had as many as three.

His heart ached at the thought of them all being away from each other. For so long, they had been there for each other. His prizes kept each other company. Now they were all alone, and one by one were going back to the families that didn't deserve them.

Everything was off-kilter this time. And patience wasn't going to stave him off.

He stopped behind an ugly potted tree and peered into the kids' jewelry and costume store. Maisie was wearing a rainbow-colored wig and twirling around in a tutu. Her mom was snapping pictures with her phone.

That was a good idea. If he couldn't get Maisie herself, he could at least look at images on his phone. On the other hand, if he waited thirty seconds, Emily would post them online.

He didn't take out his phone. Just kept watching her, spinning and laughing. She was a beautiful child. Such a happy spirit. Definitely different from the others. She needed to be taken away before she turned into one of *them*. Domineering, rude, bossy women. Always demanding their own way. The worst part was how young they turned that way these days. It had to be all the hormones in the food. The government was trying to send everyone to an early death. Aging everyone faster. Making kids lose their childhoods early. Ruining sweet little girls.

The longer Maisie played ballerina, the more Tony found himself relaxing. She was like a tiny angel.

He couldn't wait to have her all to himself. What a pleasure that would be. He wouldn't have to share her any longer. Finally, a little girl who would keep her lovely disposition.

Emily put her phone away and said something to her daughter. Maisie's expression fell. Her mom said something else, then the girl squirmed out of the tutu and put it up, then removed the wig and put it back.

Tony took a deep breath. Maybe the woman would finally take her eyes off Maisie for a moment and give him his opportunity.

His skin was on fire. He couldn't wait another day. School was impossible. There was no way he would get her there. Not unless she was one of those kids who walked home—then he could get her before or after. But so few kids did that these days.

Stupid helicopter parents. They made life so difficult on everyone. Taking kids used to be so much easier.

Maisie and her mom left the jewelry store with a little white baggie. The girl swung it back and forth, skipping ahead of her mom.

Tony held back a moment before following them. Couldn't make it obvious. Especially not with those blasted cameras everywhere. He really missed the simpler times. Thirty years before had been the golden age. Kids Maisie's age went off on their own all the time, and nobody thought anything of it. But to be fair, it was people like Tony who had ruined that. Parents didn't want their kids taken away. Not that it changed the fact that they deserved it. Raising spoiled, bossy brats.

There were still ways to get kids. There were always ways. He had proved that time and time again. He just needed to keep getting smarter along with the society and technology that made it more of a challenge.

The hunt was half the fun. It made the capture all the sweeter.

Up ahead, Maisie stopped and pointed to a shop. Tony couldn't see what kind of a store it was from how far back he was. He pretended to look at some space-age glasses at a kiosk, while Maisie pleaded with her mom.

Emily held her ground, then the two walked on.

Tony nodded to the kiosk attendant and chased after Maisie and her mom, careful not to lose them and to keep from drawing any attention to himself.

He slowed when he reached the spot Maisie had been begging.

A pet store. Kittens played in a large display, chasing after each other and hiding behind tall climbers.

Tony glanced back at Maisie and her mom. They disappeared around a corner.

He let them.

This was his answer. The present in his car wasn't quite enough. A kitty, however, would be more than enough. And since Maisie was going to be his forever girl, the expense would be worth it.

He smiled as he watched the little fur balls jump, pounce, and slide across the floor. It was anyone's guess which one had captured Maisie's heart.

Any of them would do the job—they were all cute baby cats. Maisie would go with him for sure. But it would be all the better if he could find the one she liked best.

It was so hard to say. They came in all colors—black, orange, white, calico, and gray. The multi-colored one had bright blue eyes that really stood out. That had to be the one.

He watched them a few more minutes just to be sure. Then he marched into the pet shop.

A teenager with a long pink ponytail gave him a tired smile. "Can I help you?"

"Yes. I'd like to see your calico cat."

TREASURE

Tony tapped his fingers on the steering wheel as the kitten meowed in the backseat. Neither car was parked in front of the house. Usually, they were both there. Ryan should be fiddling with his motorcycle and Emily should be inside, posting pictures of dinner and her nails.

Where could they be? He'd lost them in his effort to purchase the cat, leaving his wallet over five-hundred dollars lighter once everything was said and done. As Tony found out, one couldn't simply buy a pet—they also needed special food, a bed, and other crap like that. But if Maisie was going to be happy with it, he was happy. Just poorer.

He glanced up and down the street. Where were they?

Then it struck him. It was Wednesday. They went to church, and a lot of churchgoers attended midweek services.

It might be easier to snatch her there than in the neighborhood. This could be to his advantage.

He started the car and drove the short distance to the church. Sure enough, the parking lot was full and plenty of lights were on inside. It was impossible to tell if Maisie's parents' vehicles were there, but they probably were since neither were at home.

Tony checked that the cat had enough water still, cracked open the back windows, then headed for the building. Gospel songs sounded from across the street in the church.

He smiled at the ushers as he slid through the front door and clapped in tune with the music. The sanctuary was full of happy, singing congregants.

Tony slid into an available space near the back, continued clapping, and tried to sing along with the song about the coming glory of Heaven. He ended up mouthing the word 'watermelon' as he scanned the crowd for Ryan and Emily.

They were in the same pew as they had been on Sunday, standing no closer to each other. Maisie was probably in the children's class.

A new song started, and Tony slid out of his seat back out to the foyer. He nodded to an usher. "Where's the bathroom?"

The cheerful thirty-something pointed him in the direction.

Tony gave a quick thanks and headed that way, hoping to find the kids' classes nearby. He reached the bathroom before a row of doors.

The usher waved to him, so Tony waved back and ducked into the restroom. He exchanged greetings with a guy washing his hands, then went to the urinal where nobody would bother him.

Once the others left, he peeked outside. The usher was clapping and singing, his attention on the sanctuary.

Tony slipped out and wandered down the hallway toward a row of doors, hopeful they were classrooms.

They were. Each door had a nice, big window. The first few classrooms had babies and toddlers, so he hurried past those until he saw kids closer to Maisie's age.

He glanced back every so often to make sure nobody was watching him. The noisy preacher's voice traveled down the hall, and the ushers were all paying attention to the sermon.

Good.

Tony slowed at each window until he finally found Maisie. She wore a yellow tutu over her pants—that had to have been what she'd gotten back at the mall.

She glanced up from the picture she was coloring and waved when she saw him.

The smile on her face warmed him through and through. Tony waved, his grin matching hers.

Maisie turned her attention back to the paper, scrawling with a serious expression.

Tony admired her for a moment before pulling himself away and heading back to the sanctuary. No need for someone to think he was a creeper. He took the same seat he'd had before and did his best to sit still. It was hard given how close he was to bringing his treasure home.

The cabin was primed and ready. Full of fresh food. Aired out and scrubbed. Clean bedding in her room.

It would be their own private paradise. The place was so far out of the way, nobody would ever find them. It was the building time had forgotten. Built by his grandfather. Ignored by his spiteful alcoholic father. Restored by Tony after he ran away as a teenager. It had been the only place he could stay, where nobody would bother him.

It was also where he eventually started bringing his treasures once he realized how much joy they brought him. He hadn't meant to kill the first few. Amy, his first girlfriend and first victim, had been a complete accident. She'd pissed him off, talking down to him like his dad always did after his mother's suicide. Blaming him for things that weren't his fault.

Everyone was always blaming him for everything. His sister's death. Then Mom's suicide. Even Dad turning to the drink. Then there was his brother. His stupid, stupid brother…

Tony took a deep breath. He wasn't here to think about them. Any of them. Life-ruining retards. He was here to bring Maisie home and finally have the happiness he deserved, that he'd been searching for all these years.

He let his mind wander back to the house—before all his treasures had been taken away. How he'd loved wandering through the yard and visiting them. Burying Amy there had been a matter of convenience since it was her home and where he'd killed her, but it ended up being a place of complete comfort.

The sermon ended. More singing.

He collected his thoughts, then got up and slid into the hallway, nodding to the usher again. He pretended to read the postings on a bulletin board while watching for Maisie's parents.

After the song, people streamed out into the foyer. Emily was one of the first. She bustled toward the classrooms. No more than two minutes later, Maisie raced into the entry and out the door, her tutu bouncing along with her blonde locks.

Emily stopped near the bathrooms and spoke with another woman.

This was it. His opportunity. Nobody was watching Maisie.

Tony stepped outside, asserting full restraint. He wanted to run after his treasure. But one wrong move could mess everything up.

Now, more than ever, he needed to make sure every move was calculated. Perfect.

Maisie ran around the grass, chasing other kids and laughing. She waved to him as she passed.

He nodded then moseyed over to an apple tree and leaned against it. A minute later, Maisie stopped in front of him and caught her breath.

"I've still got that present." Tony kept his tone nonchalant, almost making it sound like he didn't care if she came to get it.

"When can I have it?"

"Anytime you want. Oh, and I have something else."

Her eyes widened. "What?"

He let a beat pass between them. "A kitten."

Maisie's eyes widened even more. "You do?"

Tony nodded. "Just got him today."

She squealed.

He looked around to make sure nobody was paying any attention. Her parents weren't outside, and the other adults were busy on their phones or talking to each other. "Want to see? He's in my car because I haven't made it home yet. You would love his bright blue eyes. I've never seen a calico with such pretty eyes."

Maisie covered her mouth. "Did you get him at the mall?"

Tony nodded.

"I was looking at that kitty! I begged Mommy for him, but she said no."

"You can play with him if you want. I don't think your parents would mind, would they? We went to lunch, remember?"

Maisie looked like she was about to explode with excitement.

"Do you want to help me name him? I can't think of anything that fits."

Her mouth dropped open. "Where's your car?"

He nodded in the direction. "I'll meet you over there in a minute, okay?"

Maisie glanced back and forth between him and the building. "I guess she won't mind if I come right back."

"Of course you can. I'll even tell her you're with me. Go ahead, and I'll meet you."

She burst into a run for the sidewalk. Nobody batted an eye.

He waited a few moments, which felt like a few eternities. Then headed toward his car, taking a path around the building, so they wouldn't be seen leaving the same way.

When he reached his car, Maisie was jumping up and down, looking inside. "He's in the kennel?"

Tony nodded, then remote unlocked his car. "Climb on in."

URGENT

"Okay, kids, time to get ready for bed." Nick glanced at the time, more than ready to get some shut-eye.

Hanna groaned and Ava glared at him. Parker didn't look up from his game.

Nick's phone rang. The ringtone told him it was someone from work. If it was anyone else, he'd ignore it. But he couldn't ignore work.

He accepted the call. "Fleshman here."

"It's Garcia. There's a kidnapping a few towns over. The missing girl matches our guy's MO."

Nick's head snapped up. "Are you sure?"

"Right age. Blonde little girl."

"Little girl?" Nick asked. "How little? Many of the vics were teenagers."

"She just turned nine. The most recent ones are all under twelve. There hasn't been a teenager in over a decade—not that's been identified yet, anyway. He seems to go for younger ones each year."

"Sick bastard," Nick muttered.

"Language, Dad." Ava smirked at him.

Nick stepped outside. "I'd better get down to the station."

"I'd say so. If this is our guy, he's going to kill her. No question about it."

"How long ago was she taken?"

"A half hour ago, from her church. I just heard about it."

"I'll be right down." Nick ended the call, then called his parents to let them know he'd be dropping the kids off for the night. He went inside. "Pack your things. You're spending the night at Grandma and Grandpa's."

"Yay!" Hanna skittered down the hall to her room.

Ava groaned. "I'm old enough to stay home alone. I can watch them."

"You mean Hanna." Parker shoved her. "I can watch myself."

She shoved him back.

Nick was about to tell them to knock it off, but he was too grateful that they were back to annoying each other again after everything they'd been through. "I'm not going to argue. If you want anything tonight or in the morning before school, pack it. You're spending the night. I'll probably be driving you straight to school from there."

They grumbled, but headed to their rooms.

Nick wandered around the house, making sure nothing was plugged in or turned on that shouldn't be. He'd likely be gone all night, catching only a little sleep on the couch in his office.

Twenty minutes later, he was kissing his children and thanking his parents. At least they understood the demands of his job and were always happy to have their grandkids over.

Another fifteen minutes, and he was at work. The air in the station was buzzing with news of a new abduction. Most everyone was in one of the conference rooms, sweets or coffee in hand. Nick glanced at the table and took a maple bar.

Anderson and Garcia stood at the front of the room, scrawling on the whiteboard as fast as they were talking.

Nick made mental notes until he finished his dessert, then

made actual notes in his phone's app. They had no description of the assailant, but several pictures of the little girl. She was adorable, and her big eyes tugged on his heartstrings.

The media would be all over this, especially in light of the killer who had buried so many bodies in Walter and Brenda's yard.

Garcia invited Nick up to the front of the room.

Nick shoved his phone into a pocket and marched up. "The likelihood of Maisie being killed is high. We need to have several people at the Foster household. But more than that, we need eyes everywhere. With any luck, the abductor will bring her to our town alive. Our first priority is getting her safe and sound. I want extra patrols out, looking for any man with a young blonde girl—or any hair color. He could change it. Not a second is to go by without an eye on the house. The rest of us are going to pore over the previous case files like never before. No clue is to be missed. Tell me about everything you find, no matter how insignificant."

They discussed the details before everyone hurried out of the conference room.

Nick went straight to his office, leaving the door open so he could hear everything. He went through his files, paying attention to details he missed before because they weren't important then. Now with a girl they could save, the case took on a whole new urgency. Sure, there was the possibility that the two cases were completely unrelated, but he had a gut-feeling that this was their guy. And that feeling had yet to be wrong.

VINDICATION

Alex sipped his peppermint mocha, then started his car. It was one of those nights he wanted to sleep in the dorm. The physical training had felt more like punishment than anything else, and everything hurt.

But Zoey really wanted to see him, and there was no way he could say no to her, especially while she was on bedrest with their child growing inside of her.

He was still trying to wrap his mind around the whole situation. One of the babies was his and one wasn't. It was like something out of a sci-fi movie.

Regardless, this was his life. He would have married and supported Zoey even if both of the babies had been Dave's.

Alex was about to pull out of the parking spot when his phone rang. He was tempted to let it go to voicemail, but he needed to answer in case it was Zoey.

It was Nick. What did he want?

"Hey, Nick. I'm just about to hit the road."

"I won't keep you. Will you stop by the station tonight?"

Alex's stomach dropped. "Why?"

"I need you to see something."

"What is it? I'm at least an hour out, and Zoey's expecting me."

"This won't take long. I just need you to see something."

"You're not going to tell me what?"

"No. I want your honest reaction when you see it."

Alex's curiosity was piqued. "Okay. Like I said, it'll be about an hour."

"See you then." The call ended.

Alex took a gulp of his coffee, not that he needed it now. His mind was racing with possibilities, his curiosity about to drive him crazy.

The drive seemed to take twice as long, but he finally pulled into the station. He texted Zoey before going in, so she'd know he was running late.

When Alex entered Nick's office, his friend didn't even look up from his stack of paperwork.

Alex cleared his throat.

Nick glanced up. "Oh, good. You're here."

"What do you want me to see?"

"Have a seat." Nick gestured to the couch, then grabbed a file and a tablet. "Have a look at this."

Alex's pulse pounded. Had he been caught doing something he wasn't supposed to? He'd been careful not to do anything stupid since starting the academy. Was it something old? Or something else altogether that had nothing to do with him?

Nick flipped through papers in the file, then handed one to Alex. "Look at this guy."

Alex's heart skipped a beat as soon as he saw what was on the paper.

He was staring at a fuzzy image of Flynn. The same man who had been following Alex, but everyone else swore was in prison. "Where'd you get this?"

"Who do you think that is?" Nick asked.

"It's Flynn. Exactly like I've been saying. Longer hair, tan, and blue eyes—but it's him."

Nick nodded. "That's what I thought."

"Now you believe me?"

"I never thought you were crazy."

"But now you know I've been seeing Flynn. Where'd you get this?"

Nick slid his finger around the tablet's screen. "We believe he's the one who took a missing nine-year-old girl."

Alex stared at him. It all made sense, except for the fact that Flynn usually took older girls.

"He's been following her family for a week. Look, here's footage of him trailing Maisie and her mom in a mall. And here he is at their church." Nick moved over to another picture. "Then he even watched them at their home on at least three nights. He was captured on two different neighbor's security cameras."

Alex's mind spun. Not only had he been right about Flynn being free, but now there was actual proof. His future coworkers would have no more reason to question his sanity.

"But that's not all."

Alex turned back to Nick. "It isn't?"

He shook his head. "The family recognized him. He introduced himself at church and took them out for lunch on Sunday."

A chill ran down Alex's spine. "Creepy much?"

"It doesn't stop there. He bought a kitten. We think that's how he finally lured Maisie away."

"What a sick piece of crap."

Nick nodded. "So, you think it's Flynn Myer?"

"Yeah, but everyone says he's at Walla Walla."

"Someone's there."

"Didn't you go there?" Alex asked. "You talked to him."

"Briefly, yes. But we all saw him in court. That was him, yet this appears to be him, too. It looks just like him."

"That's what I've been saying all along!" Realization struck Alex. "Twins."

"What?" Nick exclaimed. "Flynn doesn't have a brother. We looked into his family history when he was arrested."

"There has to be an explanation. Separated at birth? I don't know, but it makes too much sense not to be true."

Nick looked deep in thought, then shook his head. "I saw his records myself—there were no other siblings. We need to get to the bottom of this. Now."

Alex pulled out his phone and went over to the texting conversation with the anonymous texter. "Flynn—if that's who's in prison—wants me to visit him."

Nick took the phone and read through the entire conversation. "Let's go."

"Now?" Alex exclaimed. "Zoey needs me. And it's going to take hours to get there. I have academy in the morning."

"I'll buy you a mocha. Can you have her mom or Macy check on her? There's a missing girl on the line."

Alex chewed on his lower lip. Was this his future? Running to solve crimes when his family needed him?

"Alex?"

"I'll check."

Nick rose and hurried to his desk. "And I'll let the prison know we're heading over."

VIGIL

Genevieve moved the curtains and glanced out the window. Again. There was another undercover cruiser outside her parents' house. That made five that she could see. There were probably more behind the house on the other road.

She went into the room that Tinsley had claimed for herself. The girl was reading her novel. She looked up and smiled.

"How are you, kiddo?" Genevieve sat on the end of the bed.

"Tired." Tinsley yawned.

"Let's get you ready for bed."

"What about the vigil?"

Genevieve's heart skipped a beat. She hadn't told Tinsley about the latest missing girl or the vigil scheduled at the little girl's church in an hour. "You know about that?"

"Yeah. I want to go."

Genevieve took a deep breath. Was it a good idea if Tinsley went? It was a school night, and she had already been exposed to way too many abductions.

"Please." Tinsley set her novel down. "Maybe it'll help."

Genevieve bit her lower lip.

"I want to help. Mom."

Genevieve's heart skipped a beat. *Mom?*

Tinsley gave her a shy smile. "Is it okay if I call you that?"

She swallowed, a mixture of both pride and fear coursing through her. "Of course."

"Then will you take me, Mom?" Tinsley scooted closer. "Please? I can go to bed later."

Genevieve nodded. "Okay. Why don't you get ready, and I'll let my parents know we're going."

"Grandma and Grandpa," Tinsley corrected, her eyes sparkling.

"Right." Genevieve's mind swam as she headed for the living room.

Her parents were watching the news. The coverage was on the missing girl. The image moved from a picture of the girl at her recent birthday party to the Foster's house.

It had taken the media no time at all to figure out the possible connection between the two cases. There was even a livestream set up at the house. It made Genevieve all the more eager to get out of the house. She and Tinsley were still staying at Nick's condo, and so far, nobody seemed to notice.

She intended to keep it that way.

"Is everything okay?" Her dad arched a brow.

"Tinsley wants to go to the vigil. Do you want to go with us?"

"You're not staying here?"

"I don't need my every move live-streamed for the curious masses. We're going back to the condo."

Her mom frowned. "I wish you'd stay here. You're safe with all the police watching this place."

Genevieve lowered her voice. "Because they expect a serial killer to come here. Do you really want to be here?"

Her dad crossed his arms. "We've been here before when he's come here to do his dirty work."

"Actually, I'm quite certain the 'dirty work' was done elsewhere.

Obviously, it's your choice what you do. But Tinsley and I are going to the vigil to show our support. It would probably look good if you did, too." She spun around and went back to the bedrooms.

Fifteen minutes later, the four of them pulled out of the driveway in two cars. Her mom and dad in his car, because they insisted on returning to the house afterward, and Genevieve and Tinsley in the other car to go to the condo later.

If she didn't know better, she might think it was just a normal night driving down her parents' street, but all she could see were cars with people watching them. Especially the van responsible for the livestream.

Now the world knew her parents' home was empty. Hopefully, everyone also knew how many officers were watching it.

The drive was peaceful and quiet, other than the undercover car following them. Her parents probably didn't notice, but Genevieve couldn't *not* notice. Not with her training.

When she arrived at the church, the parking lot was full. They parked on the street a few blocks away.

"Is this really safe?" her dad muttered. "With a killer on the loose?"

"We're fine, Dad. It's a crowd."

"A little girl was taken from here last night."

Genevieve glanced at Tinsley, then glared at him. "Would you stop? Everything is *fine*."

He shrugged, and at least kept quiet for the rest of the short walk.

Once they arrived at the church, someone handed them candles and *Missing* fliers. Someone spoke about the little girl, then prayed. The group sang several songs before others spoke.

Genevieve put an arm around Tinsley, who rested her head against Genevieve's shoulder.

Someone handed out warm drinks, then the girl's parents spoke, pleading with everyone to find their only daughter.

The pain in their voices broke Genevieve's heart. She tried blinking back tears, but couldn't.

A few more people spoke and prayed before one last song. Hardly anyone moved, speaking quietly with those around them.

Tinsley yawned.

Genevieve turned to her parents. "I'm going to get her home."

"You mean to the condo?" Her dad lifted a brow.

"Right. You guys should go straight home. No fishing."

His expression tightened. "I know. I'm staying within sight until all of this is over."

They said their goodbyes, then Genevieve and Tinsley headed back to her car.

Someone followed them.

She met his gaze, and he showed his badge.

Hopefully it was real. The man at least kept his distance.

When they got to the car, Genevieve pulled out her keys. The phone fell out, and she caught it. It showed a voice message.

Her first thought was, maybe it was Nick. But that was unlikely. He would be swamped with the case. Close to half his force was parked outside her parents' house.

Once locked inside the car, she checked the message.

"What is it?" Tinsley asked. "You look happy."

"I am." She'd just been offered a job at a nearby precinct. Once this case was over, they would be in the clear to date. It would be smart to give it a little more time before announcing anything, but they could soon tell the world how they felt about each other.

SPIRAL

Maisie sat curled in a ball on the couch, crying and clinging to the kitten. She'd been doing that most of the day.

Nothing Tony did helped. She had no interest in any of the toys or games he'd bought for her. Didn't care about the pretty, girly room just for her. None of that mattered. She barely appreciated the cat.

Neither one of them had eaten or slept since arriving at the cabin. In a full day.

He took a deep breath. "Come *on*. You've got to eat."

She shook her head and rubbed her tear-streaked face.

"I thought you'd love it here. Nobody to bother you or make you feel bad. You didn't have to put up with those brats from school. How many of them got to spend the day with such a cute kitten?"

Tears ran down her face and her lips trembled. "I want my mommy."

"No, you don't!"

She sniffled and buried her face into the cat's fur.

"You'll feel better after you eat. I'm going to warm up the food you refused earlier."

He ignored her sobs as he made his way over to the kitchen and put her plate in the microwave. His stomach rumbled. He wasn't going to eat until she did, but if she continued refusing, he might have to have a meal by himself.

Maisie continued crying while he waited for her food to warm.

He clenched his fists, then pulled out his phone to check the updates. The kidnapping was still top news, trending everywhere above most everything else, although a tsunami was threatening some random island and that story was gaining traction.

"Come on, tsunami," he mumbled.

The microwave beeped. He put away the phone and pulled out the steaming plate of macaroni and cheese with animal-shaped chicken nuggets and mashed potatoes. Foods that every kid loved.

He set it next to her. "Eat. You need your strength."

The kitten sniffed at it, more interested than Maisie.

"When can I go home?"

"Don't you like this place?"

"I wanna go home, Tony."

He gritted his teeth. "This place is better than home. You have a kitty, you have all those toys in your bedroom, and now you have the biggest yard ever—the whole forest!"

"But not my parents."

"They're always dropping you off places. At daycare, school, class at church. Really, how often do you actually see them? I have all the time in the world for you. You can do whatever you want. Anything!"

She finally met his gaze. "I want to see my mommy and daddy. I want to go home and ride my Hummer."

"That's what you're worried about?" He exclaimed. "I'll get you a whole fleet of cars you can ride! You won't be limited to the sidewalk. You can ride those things all over the forest. Literally anywhere you want."

Maisie frowned.

Anger was starting to build in his chest. "Look. You need to eat. Clean that plate, or I'll give you something to really cry about!"

More tears spilled onto her face.

Tony spun around and stormed into the kitchen. He was starting to sound like his dad, and he hated that. The last person he wanted to turn into was that monster—the man who blamed his wife's suicide on his two sons. It wasn't like he could blame it on their dead sister.

Raw fury ran through him at the thought of it all. He'd run away as a teenager, never to return home, but that didn't stop all of those old events from haunting him. They would never leave him alone. His father's harsh words would follow him to the grave. Nothing could make him forget.

He could pretend they never happened, but he was only kidding himself. There was no forgetting his dad, ever.

Maisie was still sniffling in the next room. "You'd better be eating! That plate better be clean by the time I get in there, or I swear I will give you something to cry about! Things here can either be really good or really bad. It's your choice!"

He piled some food on a plate and stuck it in the microwave, slamming the door.

The girl was still making noises in the living room.

It rubbed his last nerve raw. He needed to calm down before he really started acting like his old man. To distract himself, he brought out his phone again. Most every news source was dominated by the kidnapping and the impending tsunami. Apparently, there was a vigil at the church for Maisie.

Like that was going to convince him to bring her back. Not when he'd gone to so much effort to get her to the cabin. It had been almost a week, and he'd spent a lot of money.

No. She was *his* now, and he'd do whatever it would take to make her feel at home and comfortable. What they both needed was food and sleep. He certainly didn't trust her enough to let himself fall asleep. No, she was a flight risk. So, after eating, he would have to lock her in the bedroom—something he hadn't wanted to do—just so he could get some shut eye. He really needed some. His eyelids were fighting to close.

The microwave beeped. He took his food and shoveled it into his mouth, not caring that it burned. After swallowing, he called to Maisie, "I'm eating, and you'd better be, too. Are you?"

"Yes."

"Good. We'll both feel a lot better."

He continued scarfing down food and checking the news feeds for updates.

Then he saw something that made him choke.

His picture.

He was now wanted in connection to Maisie's disappearance. Interviews with the girl's parents, the church usher, the girl at the pet shop, and even the waiter from the restaurant he'd eaten at with Maisie's family all described him in detail.

No... he hadn't been careful enough. But it didn't matter. Nobody would ever be able to find him in the cabin. It was a place the world had forgotten. The building may as well not even exist as far as anyone else was concerned.

He put his plate and fork in the sink. "Time for bed, Maisie. We need our sleep. It's going to be a busy day tomorrow."

ANSWERS

Alex's pulse pounded as he stared at the small, nondescript room. It was even more plain and more intimidating than the interrogation rooms back at their precinct.

Nick flipped through a pad of paper, seemingly at ease in the penitentiary. Two guards were on their way with Flynn—or whoever was in death row in his place. It felt like forever since they'd left for him. They had to be close.

Would Alex finally get the answers he'd been in search of for so long? Could he tell Flynn everything he had been wanting to say since the man had taken Ariana?

The door opened.

Alex sat up straight and exchanged a glance with Nick. They both wanted answers, but this was personal for Alex. This man had been toying with Alex for too long.

The two guards shoved Flynn into the room and secured him to the other side of the table. He was cuffed at his wrists and ankles, and the cuffs were connected with thick chain.

Flynn glared at Alex. The man had his thinning hair again, and his skin was as pale as it had been before. His blue eyes were also dark again. But it was definitely him.

The guards said they'd be just outside if needed, then left.

It took every bit of Alex's self-control to stay in the chair as he stared at the man who had abducted Ariana. He clenched his fists under the table and glared at the criminal. "What's going on?" he demanded. "Why did you want to see me?"

Flynn leaned back, a smug expression covering his face. "Whatever do you mean?"

Alex glanced at Nick, who gave him a look reminding him to stay calm. Alex gritted his teeth.

"Well?" Flynn smirked.

"Will you stop with the texts after this?" Alex demanded.

"What texts?"

Alex leaned forward. "You know what texts!"

Flynn shrugged.

Nick pressed his palms on the table. "If you don't want to talk about that, we can always discuss the missing girl. Where is she?"

"What missing girl? I don't hear much news in the slammer, you know. I've been here for, what, two years now? It's so hard to tell. Time just isn't the same in here."

"Boohoo." Alex glared at him and took a deep breath. "You wanted me here. Why?"

The jerk's expression turned smug again. "I hear you're blaming things on me that I haven't done."

"We have pictures." Nick slid a zoomed-in picture of Flynn with Maisie and her family that had been in the background of someone else's photo.

Flynn studied it. "Looks like Flynn is up to his old games."

Alex gave Nick a knowing look before turning to Flynn. "So you *do* have a twin!"

He pointed to the picture and smirked again. "That would be Flynn."

If Alex could get away with punching the psycho, he'd do it in a heartbeat.

"If he's Flynn, who the hell are you?" Nick asked, keeping his expression rigid.

Flynn shrugged.

"Who are you?" Alex struggled not to yell. "If you're not Flynn, who *are* you?"

"Lloyd, the better-looking brother. Everyone just assumed I was Flynn when I was arrested for my murders, so I went with it." He yawned. "My brother isn't happy with me taking his fake identity, but whatever."

Alex could hardly believe he'd been right about the twin theory. "You're Lloyd?"

"Yes. Flynn is my twin. And yes, I know that rhymes—Flynn the twin. I've always hated that, but it is what it is."

"And you *both* kidnap and murder girls?" Alex couldn't wrap his mind around it.

Flynn—Lloyd—glanced down at the photograph. "Apparently. I didn't know he was in the game, too. He knew what I was doing but never said anything about his activities. The snide loser always acted like he was better than me. Turns out he's not. Can't say I'm surprised, actually."

Nick flipped through his pages of notes. "So, you're Lloyd Myer and your brother—?"

"Lloyd *Vassman*. Myer was Flynn's fake identity. Changed his name after Dad kicked him out of the house. Dad was damn near ready to kill Flynn after everything that happened."

"Everything? What happened?" Alex demanded.

Lloyd's expression darkened. "Our sister died accidentally. After that, Mom did herself in. Dad turned to alcohol and blamed me and Flynn. My brother high-tailed it out of there. I stuck around and listened to him blaming me for everything until I graduated and escaped. Then I started recreating our sister's death and killing the girls for not cooperating. Now I'm here—but you already knew that."

Nick mumbled to himself, flipping through his pages and also sliding his finger around his phone's screen. Then he looked up at Lloyd. "So, it was because of the fake last name that we never discovered you were a twin."

"Bingo." Lloyd gave him a Cheshire grin.

"I see it all here. Do you know what assumed name Flynn is using now? Everyone seems to think his name is Tony."

Lloyd snorted. "The loser took Dad's name? Wow, I don't even know what to say about that."

"Where does he have the girl?" Nick stared Lloyd down.

"Do I look like I know? I've been in here for years. We've never been close, even when we were both free killers."

"Where is he?" Nick slammed his fist on the table.

"Let me check my crystal ball. Oh, wait. I don't have one."

"Where do you think he would take her?"

"His house?"

"Nope. The authorities already searched his apartment. His girlfriend told them where he lived."

"That doesn't surprise me. Flynn always needs a woman. He's pathetic that way."

"You had all kinds of properties." Nick glared at Lloyd. "Is there one he might use? One that we never found when investigating your crimes?"

"How would I know?"

Nick drew in a deep breath. "Fill in the details, or I'll call the guards back in."

"I'm done here, anyway. Good luck finding Flynn. He's evaded capture all this time. He always gets what he wants. You probably won't find him now. However, there is one cabin I never used. Have fun locating it." Lloyd hollered for the guards.

Nick told them about Lloyd's real identity. He and Alex headed back to the car, and Nick called Anderson, filling him in on everything Lloyd had told them.

LOCATION

Nick blinked his eyes several times to see the laptop screen straight. His vision was blurry from so little sleep. He'd only slept a few hours total, and on his couch, no less.

Now that they knew the truth about Flynn and Lloyd Vassman, there was so much more to work with, which also meant more time poring over details.

Everything Lloyd had told them held up—the twins, their sister, their mother, and their alcoholic father who was now also deceased.

His phone rang. It was the precinct in Maisie's town.

"Captain Fleshman."

"This is Detective Ines. We have a possible location on that cabin. There are some old paper records of it, owned by the Vassmans' dad. It was reported destroyed and never rebuilt."

Nick grabbed a pen. "What's the address?"

"The middle of the woods." Ines gave him coordinates, then filled him in on the plan to stake out the building.

"Are the feds leading this?"

"They're providing resources and working with us, but my chief is calling the shots."

"I'm going to bring in my guys."

"Good. I'll be in touch with more details."

They ended the call, then Nick scrambled out of his office and called everyone into the main conference room. He filled them in, gave orders, then raced back to his office to prepare for the drive.

Nick drove while Garcia kept in contact with the other department. It sounded like they were all going to arrive at about the same time.

Nick's heart raced. They'd already passed the critical forty-eight-hour period. Chances of saving Maisie were growing slimmer by the minute—and they were dealing with a man who killed all of his victims. Just like his twin brother.

What were the chances of twin serial killers? Was it in the DNA, or the way they'd been raised? Perhaps a mixture of both. Everything they'd gone through in their early teen years would've been enough to cause severe psychological damage to anyone. But not everyone would turn to murdering girls. There had to be something in their biological make-up that drove them to it.

Nick shuddered at the thought, especially given his son could be biologically related to a psychopath.

"You okay, Captain?" Garcia asked.

"Yeah. Just hoping we can save the girl. If he knows we're on to him, he might move faster to hurt her."

"There hasn't been any activity at the Foster house. He hasn't returned to bury her. That's good news."

"He could be waiting. Or found somewhere new to bury this one."

"He's been using the same location for thirty years. I can't see him changing now."

"There's a livestream on that house. If he knows about that, there's no way he's setting foot anywhere near there."

"That's true."

"And all his other victims are gone. The Foster's property

means nothing to him now. People like him return to relive their past conquests."

"In that case, let's hope this cabin is it, and that the girl is safe."

Nick glanced at the time. "All we can do is hope."

The GPS unit instructed him to turn down a barely-visible dirt road nestled in between thick trees.

By the time they reached the end of the road, more than a dozen other vehicles were already parked there. Some officers mingled near a van.

Nick and Garcia went over to the group. More vehicles barreled down the trail and parked. The others brought Nick and Garcia up to speed.

Officers and agents were scouring the area for the cabin, or anywhere Flynn might be hiding with the girl.

Nick and Garcia headed out in a direction nobody else had gone yet. Silence fell around them, and the only sounds were of their breathing and of twigs snapping beneath their feet.

The trail grew tighter, and they used their knives to cut prickly vines while balancing their flashlights. Several thorns cut Nick as he made his way through.

Garcia kicked down a branch in their way. "Doesn't seem like anyone's been out this way in a long time. Maybe we should turn back. There's no way a man and a kid came through this."

"They might've taken a different route, but I say we keep going until we can't."

"It's your call."

An owl hooted not far away.

"If that isn't creepy, I don't know what is." Garcia cut another vine.

"Maybe it means we're close."

"If you say so."

The path grew thicker, and it got to the point where Nick was about ready to turn around.

Then they came to an opening.

He and Garcia exchanged a curious glance then walked through a small field which led to another tight path.

Garcia groaned. "I say we go back."

Nick pulled out his phone and slid his finger around the screen until he found what he was looking for. "We're practically on top of the coordinates for that cabin."

"I'm sure we are." Garcia took a deep breath. "Let's do this."

They made their way along the small path, chopping things out of their way and earning more cuts in the process.

"We really should go back," Garcia said. "This isn't getting us anywhere."

Nick squinted into the distance. "Have a look."

Garcia squeezed next to Nick and leaned forward. He swore, then turned to Nick. "Is that what I think it is?"

"A cabin. With lights on inside."

"I'll call it in."

"And I'll keep cutting these vines." Nick pushed his way through, keeping his eye on the tiny building in the distance.

The profile of a man passed by the window.

"We've got you, Flynn Vassman."

MISTAKE

~~~~

Flynn pulled on his hair, and the hairpiece came loose.

Maisie cried out and pulled the kitten closer. The cat hissed and jumped from her lap, scurrying away.

Flynn yanked the fake hair all the way off and chucked it across the room.

The little girl buried her face into a throw pillow and wailed.

"I told you to stop!"

She shook and sobbed all the more.

Everything spun around him. He stormed out of the living room and back into the laundry room where he kept his police scanner. It had picked up more activity in the last hour, and that concerned him. He hadn't been able to understand anything said, but the fact that it picked up anything was bad news.

Nobody should be anywhere near the hidden, forgotten cabin.

He turned up the volume. Static grew louder but so did the indiscernible voices. But they seemed to be becoming slightly clearer.

Then he heard something that sent a cold chill down his spine.

Nestled in between mumbles and static, he heard "Vassman" clear as day.

They knew his given last name.

His stomach dropped to the floor. The authorities knew who he was. Not just his fake identities, but who he really was. Flynn Vassman. A name he'd left behind many years earlier. A name that had died along with the guy so hated by his impossible-to-please father.

Not only that, but the cops were within earshot. They were closing in on him.

They knew where he was. They'd found the cabin. Or at least had a general idea where it was. And they knew who he was—obviously, that was something they were keeping from the public. It hadn't shown up on any of the news sources.

And Maisie was in the other room, sobbing.

Could things be any worse?

He needed more time. The girl needed more convincing. She needed food. Maybe another kitten. Or another girl to give her company? But she was one in a million. It would take forever to find another like her. And even then, he might have two inconsolable kids to deal with.

The police scanner made more noise. More words came in clearly.

They were close, and moving closer.

He needed to get out of the cabin. Now. Maisie would just have to deal with it. He would have to continue trying to pamper her later. After the cops left.

Flynn turned off the light and went around the cabin, turning them all off. No need to advertise his whereabouts.

"Why is it dark?" Maisie sniffled, still at the couch.

"We're going on an adventure."

"Home?" Hope sparked in her voice.

"This is home now." Irritation flared in his tone.

More sobs.

The police scanner continued making noise in the back. It grated on his last frayed nerve.

Flynn clenched his jaw. "Come on. We're leaving."

"I want my Mommy!"

"That's going to have to wait. We need to leave. Now!"

"Take me home. I don't like it here."

"You don't even like the cat? I got him just for you!"

"I just wanna go home," she wailed.

A whole sentence came through the police scanner, clear enough to understand every damning word. They were closing in on Flynn Vassman.

That name sent a shiver down his spine. Flynn Vassman was dead. Dead! He was now Tony Howell. That wouldn't matter to the cops.

All they would see was Flynn Vassman.

"Come on!" He stepped closer to Maisie.

"No."

"You don't tell me 'no'!" Flynn grabbed her arm and yanked her to her feet. "We're leaving, and you're going to stop arguing. Got it?"

She squirmed. "You're hurting me."

He squeezed harder. "Do you understand me?"

"Ow! Yes."

"Yes, what?" he snapped.

"I understand!" Maisie pulled away from him.

"You need to do as I say, or someone's going to get killed."

She froze. "Y-you're going to kill me?"

"That's the last thing I want. There are some bad guys coming to the cabin, and we need to get out of here."

"Bad guys?"

"Yes. There's no telling what they'll do. I want to keep you safe. To protect you. But I can only do that if you listen to me. I'm the only one who can save you."

She stopped squirming. "Y-you are?"

"Yes, but you have to do what I say. Or the bad guys might win."

Maisie stepped closer to him. "Okay."

She was finally agreeing? Maybe this was all for the best. She was finally starting to trust him.

"Stay right here. I need to get my gun."

Maisie gasped.

"To keep you safe."

"Where's the kitty?"

"I don't know. Just stay quiet." He released her arm and stormed into the other room to shut off the scanner. They were after him—point taken.

Then he grabbed a pistol and a revolver from the cabinet. It wasn't much against the mob of badges headed his way, but he could at least do some damage. They would have on protective vests, but if he aimed for the legs, he could at least put them out of commission.

His eyes were adjusting to the dark, but he couldn't see Maisie in the living room.

"Where'd you go?"

She didn't answer.

He swore under his breath. "Answer me!"

She didn't.

"I'm not playing around. You want the bad men to get you?"

Why had he let her out of sight? He never should've left the room.

He tucked the guns into his clothes and marched through the cabin. It wasn't like there were many places to hide.

"Maisie."

Silence.

"We need to leave, and we need to leave now."

Nothing.

"It's going to go a lot better for you if you come here. If I find you hiding, things aren't going to go your way."

She didn't reply.

He should've known better than to trust a female. Didn't

matter the age—they were all the same. Never listened. Never did as they were told. Bossy and arrogant.

Anger churned in his gut. It bubbled over and pulsated through his body.

He clutched his gun and crept toward the hall. "Come out, come out, wherever you are."

His skin crawled, knowing how close the cops were. It was almost tempting to leave without the girl, but he wasn't going to give her up. He'd worked too hard for her. Didn't matter that she was being obstinate. He could work with that. She'd come around. He'd make sure of it.

First, he had to find her.

He flung open the bathroom door. It banged on the wall and bounced back toward him. He stopped it before it slammed into him.

Flynn used his phone as a flashlight and shone it around the tiny room. Maisie wasn't there, unless she was hiding. There were two places she could be. Either behind the shower curtain or under the sink. Under the sink would be tight, so he crept toward the tub.

He flung the curtain out of the way.

The shower was empty.

He spun around and yanked open the cabinet door. Only his father's ancient, decrepit toiletries.

"Come out, come out, wherever you are."

The kitten scrambled down the hall. It came from Maisie's room.

Flynn sauntered toward the room. He stepped inside and shone the light around. Nothing in sight.

Haggard breathing sounded near the bed.

"Found you."

FIGHT

Flynn stepped into the room, listening to the heavy breathing. He still couldn't see the girl. She was there. Oh, she was definitely there.

"It'd be a lot better for you if you come out. I know you're in here."

She didn't emerge from her spot.

"So be it. I'll find you. Then you'll wish you'd listened. Last chance."

Nothing.

"Have it your way." He lumbered toward the closet and yanked the door open. Just his collection of clothes and shoes. All things he'd picked up along the way—some bought for girls, others left from girls.

Flynn spun around. "I'm getting closer."

Her breathing grew louder. She had to be under the bed.

"This is your very last chance. If I find you, you'll wish you'd showed yourself."

Silence. She had to be holding her breath.

"If that's the way you want it." He took small, deliberate steps toward the bed.

Gasps and heavy breaths sounded from under the bed. Ruffling noises as she scooted over the carpet.

Time was short with the cops heading his way. But he was going to make her pay for refusing to obey by making her quake with anticipation. She would regret it. Oh, how she would regret it. Both now and later.

"Are you under the bed, Maisie?"

The scooting stopped.

"Don't you know that's where the monsters live? They lie in wait for little children—to gobble them up!" He pulled up the covers.

She cowered back near the wall.

"Come out."

"No!"

He shone the light in her eyes. "I told you not to say that!"

"Go away!"

"You don't understand how this works. I'm the boss. You do what I say. Not the other way around. Get out." He motioned for her to climb out.

She shook her head.

Fury drummed through his body. "This is your last warning."

Maisie scooted back, pressing herself against the wall.

"Have it your way, then." Flynn reached for her, his fingertips barely missing her.

She cried out and moved closer to the corner.

He squeezed beneath the bed and grabbed her arm.

The little brat scratched and hit him.

Flynn yanked her, dragging her out from under the bed. "I told you you'd regret that!"

"Ow!" She twisted and squirmed.

"Now you're going to listen to me."

Maisie struggled harder than ever. Flynn lost his grip for a moment, but managed to grab the collar of her shirt.

She gagged, then kicked at him.

He called her a derogatory name, then dug out his pocket knife from his pants and flipped out the blade.

Maisie froze in place.

"See this?"

She didn't respond.

"Do you see this?" Flynn shouted.

The girl nodded and swallowed.

"Should I use this on you?"

She shook her head furiously.

He pressed it to the front of her neck. "I don't want to, but if you force me to, I will. Understand?"

"Y-yes."

"Finally." He closed the blade and stuck it back into his pocket. "We're going outside, and if you don't do what I say, you're going to find out just how sharp that knife is. Got it?"

Maisie nodded.

"Good."

Bang!

Flynn froze.

Maisie screamed.

Bang!

It took him a moment to realize what the noise was. At first, it almost sounded like a tree falling on the cabin. But it was the door.

And they weren't knocking.

Bang!

They were going to break down the door.

Flynn swore, tightened his grip around Maisie's arm, and dragged her out of the room.

Bang!

She screamed again.

He covered her mouth.

The brat bit him.

He pulled away and shook out his hand.

She hollered. It was the most high-pitched sound he'd ever heard.

Bang!

Shards of wood flew in all directions as the door shattered. Uniformed men burst inside.

Maisie yelled out.

Flynn had two choices. Leave the girl and run, or threaten her life. She was nothing more than a bargaining chip now.

The cabin had to be surrounded. That left him with only one option.

He whipped out the knife and held the blade to the girl's neck. "Make another move, and she dies!"

Several men pointed guns at him.

"Don't believe me?" He dug the blade into her skin just enough to draw blood.

She screamed like he was killing her. In fact, some of those he'd killed had made less noise. The sound would be soothing if it weren't for the guns aimed at him.

Flynn shoved her back, dropped the knife, then reached for his two guns as he jumped behind a wall.

He wasn't sure who shot first, but gunfire rang out through the air. His bullets went straight for limbs. Several men went down, but that didn't stop them from firing at him from the ground.

Flynn used up all his bullets before spinning around and running away. If he could just make it to the kitchen, he could escape. Run outside into the trees and never be seen again. He knew the hiding places. He'd used them to hide from his dad during his drunken rages.

A sharp, hot pain exploded in his shoulder. It radiated out in all directions.

Flynn stumbled, but kept going. They weren't going to take him down. He would die before he would go to jail.

Another burst of agony shattered his right knee. Then his arm.

Warm liquid soaked into his clothes.

This was it. Everything was over.

He spun around and smirked through the torment. His knee threatened to give out, but he wouldn't let it. Not yet. He wasn't going to the hospital, and he certainly wasn't going to prison.

"You think you've won? You haven't!" He aimed an empty gun at the cops.

Searing pain shot through his chest. The breath left his lungs. He couldn't stand up any longer.

The ground sailed toward him. He landed with a great crash. Everything hurt all the more.

Warm, sticky blood pooled on the floor with a metallic odor.

Shouting and chaos ensued around him.

Everything faded away into whiteness.

Nothing hurt anymore.

ILLUSION

Alex closed his eyes and held the peppermint mocha in his mouth for a moment before swallowing. He opened his eyes and looked around the table. Zoey sat next to him, and Nick and Genevieve sat across from them, holding hands.

In the next room, the kids all crowded around the TV, watching a live concert and singing along.

He couldn't believe Flynn was actually dead. That meant no more texts or phone calls. No more people thinking Alex was crazy for claiming the guy was walking around free.

It all made sense now that they knew the truth about Lloyd and Flynn Vassman, the serial killer twins.

But even more important than Flynn being out of Alex's life was the fact that Zoey was now off bedrest. The bleeding had stopped long enough for her to walk around, but she still couldn't go to work or do much else. Hopefully soon.

Someone's phone rang. Nick pulled out his and looked at the screen. "What does Garcia want? I told him I'm not going in under any circumstances today." He groaned then tapped the screen and held it to his ear. "Fleshman here."

Nick nodded a few times in response to who he was talking to, then his face paled.

"What is it?" Alex exclaimed.

Nick thanked Garcia, then turned to Alex and Zoey.

"What's the matter?" Genevieve asked.

"Lloyd hanged himself after hearing about his brother."

"He's dead?" Zoey asked.

Nick nodded. "Now that whole twisted family is gone."

Alex's mind raced as he tried to take in the news. Both of the murdering psychopaths were dead.

That meant with Dave safely in prison, Alex and Zoey could get married and rest easy. They would have nobody else to worry about.

Alex would soon be a police officer with a steady job and income. They would be married and raising a family together. One child wouldn't be his, but only biologically. The child would need a father. A family. And he or she would get that, and hopefully enough love to make up for screwed-up genetics.

Genevieve shuffled the deck of cards in front of her. "Anyone want to play a new round? It's pretty quiet around this table."

They agreed to play. Alex couldn't have been happier about the quiet afternoon.

Zoey looked at Nick. "Have you heard how that little girl who was abducted is doing?"

"I spoke with her mom yesterday. She says Maisie is doing great now. Bounced back after a couple days. That little kitten she got from the cabin has really helped a lot."

"Oh, good. I'm so glad."

"What about Flynn's other victims? Have they been identified? I hope their families have closure."

Nick nodded. "All but one. We have one Jane Doe that we're working on."

His phone rang again.

Alex frowned. "Maybe you should put that thing on silent."

"Sounds like a good idea." He reached for the screen, but his thumb froze in place as he stared at it, his face paling again.

"What now?" Alex put his arm around Zoey. "More good news?"

Nick glanced up, a mixture of worry and anger crossing his expression.

Alex's chest tightened. "What is it?"

He held out the text message. "Mason. Nobody knows where he is. He's probably headed out this way."

"Mason?" Alex exclaimed. "As in, Dave's son?"

Nick glanced over at Ava, who Mason violated while thinking she was going to be his stepsister. Nick nodded.

Alex closed his eyes. Mason was also the half-brother of Zoey's other child. Corrine and Dave's son. "Are you sure he's headed this way?"

Nick turned to him. "Can you think of anywhere else he'd go?"

Alex exchanged a glance with Zoey. The kid would be half-brother to one of Zoey's babies. Alex turned his attention back to Nick. "What are we going to do?"

"I'm going to let everyone at the precinct know to keep a lookout for him. I'll have to keep Ava close to me and let her know what's going on. In the meantime, we'll have to come up with other safeguards.

Alex took a deep breath and nodded. "For all we know, he's not coming here. Maybe he has some girlfriend he's moving closer to."

"Maybe." Nick didn't look like he believed it any more than Alex did.

YOU MAY ENJOY...

If you're enjoying the Alex Mercer series, you'll probably also really like my novel, *Dex*. I think that if Dex and Alex were to meet, they would become fast friends. They're similar in many ways—though in very different life circumstances! One thing they do have in common is that they have both spent time in Silverly. Remember the mental hospital where Saige took Alex? You'll find it in Dex, too, though a little more dilapidated. (I enjoy throwing in Easter eggs like that into my stories!)

Excerpt

Dex Sheahan held his breath and readied his bow. He stepped back, inching away from the dozen or so insatiable wanderers. They growled, hissed, and reached out, scratching one another but not finding Dex. The rancid odor of rotting flesh and exposed internal organs made his eyes water, but he held still. They would soon forget about him and move on as long as they couldn't find him.

The zombies were nothing if not predictable. Chase after anything with warm internal organs and fresh brains. Rip them out and eat. Repeat. They were strong, but incapable of intelligence. And that was how Dex had managed to live as long as he had—he used his brain, unlike so many other people he'd run in to over the years. Use it or lose it. That was the law of life in the wild.

How many years had he managed to survive? His guess was close to eleven years, but it was only that. A guess. He'd lost count of how many cold winters and hot summers had passed since escaping the safety of the tiny town he'd grown up in. But if he was right, he'd spent exactly half his life on his own, fighting to live.

The groans and grunts grew quieter. Several of the wanderers stumbled away in the opposite direction. They meandered without direction, which was no doubt how they had earned the name.

Dex released a quiet sigh of relief. The others would soon follow suit. Then he could carry on his way and find a place to sleep for the night. With any luck, it would be better than the tree branch that had been his bed the night before. It hadn't been his worst night of rest, but there was nothing like finding an old bed or couch to crash onto, no matter how lumpy or stiff.

Growl.

His heart skipped a beat. That hadn't been one of the monsters. It was his stomach.

Growl-growl.

Several of the wanderers turned his way and reached into the bush that separated them from him.

Crack. A branch broke in two.

Dex swore. Why now? It was surprises like that which would get him killed like so many other before him.

Cracked yellow claws reached for him. Growls and hisses grew louder as the creatures inched closer.

He tightened his grip on the arrow, aimed his bow at the nearest head, and released. It flew the short distance and burst into the monster's temple. It—Dex never referred to them as he or she, despite what they once had been—cried out and fell to the ground. Three more pushed through the thick bushes, snatching at him.

He reached into his quiver and readied another arrow. Unfortunately, he was running low on ammo. He hadn't had much time lately to make more or go back for the ones he'd shot. He had four, but five chased him.

Dex backed into a tree, stopping him from going any farther. His heart raced. He would need to either kill two with one shot or run from the last one. His only other option was to pull out one of his knives, but that would be a last resort. Using a blade meant allowing them close enough to bite or scratch him. If that happened, he would soon turn into one of those mindless freaks of nature.

He shot an arrow at the nearest one and again hit it directly in the temple. After an over-dramatic display of hissing and thrashing, it finally fell to the ground. Dex maneuvered around the tree while pulling out the rest of the arrows. He used each one in rapid-fire succession.

The remaining wanderer raced for him, growling and snapping. This one was fast, which meant it was especially hungry. A dirty, torn floral dress hung in tatters off its shoulders. Maybe the garment would impede its reach enough that Dex would stand a fighting chance with a knife.

Dex slung the crossbow over his shoulder and reached for his longest blade. It was seventeen inches from tip to handle and had once belonged to his dad. It would have to be good enough.

Behind the fast zombie, a group of three more headed his way. All the noise from the ones he'd just killed had gotten their attention.

Dex took a deep breath and focused on the one in front of him. It moved faster with each step. Definitely hungry for his organs.

The trees and other plant life were especially thick, making his getaway all the more challenging. He kept his attention on the rapidly-approaching creature while trying to map an escape. It was never easy, but this time would prove extra difficult with the thick trees and poison oak blocking his way.

He stepped back, barely avoiding the itchy plant, and bumped into another tree. All the branches were higher than he could reach, and the bark too smooth for him to scale. His breathing grew labored. The three behind this one closed in.

Dex stumbled over a rock. He reached down, picked it up, and threw it at the monster's face. It flinched and hissed, clawing at the air. While it was distracted, he ran past it, barely getting by. Then he rushed past the other three, careful to stay out of reach.

Dex came to a new-growth tree. It was too weak to climb, but it had plenty of branches. He ripped a few off. They weren't arrows or spears, but they would have to do. The group of three was now closer, so he turned to them and dug the pointed end of the longest branch into the nearest temple. The creature flailed about and hissed, but crumbled to the ground.

One of the zombies behind it tripped and face-planted onto a stone. Pieces of flesh and gray matter—though it was yellow and red—splattered out, some landing on Dex's pants. It wasn't the first and wouldn't be the last. The last of the group lumbered toward Dex, staring with hollow eyes and grasping for him with long ragged nails. A torn t-shirt barely hung to its body with the phrase *World's Greatest Dad* scrawled across the blood-spattered front.

"Not anymore." Dex ran at it and aimed another branch into the wanderer's temple. The thing screeched, spraying something orange onto Dex's shirt and snapped its few remaining teeth at him. Before Dex could dig the weapon into the skull, the zombie reached out for him. Dex jumped out of the way and missed getting scratched by less than an inch.

His heart jumped into his throat. He hadn't had a close call like that in some time. Dex raised a foot and pulled his leg close to his body before side-kicking the thing in its stomach and then knees. It reached for Dex, hissing, as it stumbled backward. The thing managed to keep its balance, proving to be more difficult to kill than its now-dead friends.

It hissed, spraying orange into the air, and marched toward Dex. The zombie in the dress had finally figured out where Dex had gone and rushed toward him, twice as fast as the world's greatest dad approached. In less than thirty seconds, he would have to fight them both off at the same time.

There was only one thing to do. He held both branches in the air, aimed them at the nearest one, and launched them with all his might. One hit the dress-zombie, who crashed into a tree with a loud thud. The world's greatest dad turned toward the noise, and Dex took advantage of its distraction. He grabbed another branch and threw it. It sailed silently through the air and smashed into the zombie's temple, shattering the skull upon impact. Dad convulsed before falling only feet from his companions.

No time to catch his breath. The dress-monster raced over, screaming and growling. As it ran toward him, intestines fell out and hung from its middle, but it didn't slow down. It bared its graying teeth and reached for him with disgusting jaundiced nails.

He aimed his last branch at the monster, but froze before throwing it. A sliver of sunlight shining through the trees reflected off the creature's necklace.

Dex recognized it. He'd seen it countless times as a boy. It was one of his family's few heirlooms. His mom never took it off. Ever.

The monster trying to kill him was his mom.

More information: https://stacyclaflin.com/books/dex/

OTHER BOOKS BY STACY CLAFLIN

If you enjoy reading outside the romance genre, you may enjoy some of Stacy Claflin's other books, also. She's a *USA Today* bestselling author who writes about complex characters overcoming incredible odds. Whether it's her Gone saga of psychological thrillers, her various paranormal romance tales, or her romances, Stacy's three-dimensional characters shine through bringing an experience readers don't soon forget.

The Gone Saga

The Gone Trilogy: Gone, Held, Over

Dean's List

No Return

Alex Mercer Thrillers

Girl in Trouble

Turn Back Time

Little Lies

Against All Odds

Don't Forget Me

Curse of the Moon

Lost Wolf

Chosen Wolf

Hunted Wolf

Broken Wolf

Cursed Wolf

Secret Jaguar

Valhalla's Curse

Renegade Valkyrie

Pursued Valkyrie

Silenced Valkyrie

Vengeful Valkyrie

The Transformed Series

Main Series

Deception

Betrayal

Forgotten

Ascension

Duplicity

Sacrifice

Destroyed

Transcend

Entangled

Dauntless

Obscured

Partition

Standalones

Fallen

Silent Bite

Hidden Intentions

Saved by a Vampire

Sweet Desire

Short Story Collection

Tiny Bites

The Hunters

Seaside Surprises

Seaside Heartbeats

Seaside Dances

Seaside Kisses

Seaside Christmas

Bayside Wishes

Bayside Evenings

Bayside Promises

Bayside Destinies

Bayside Opposites

Bayside Chances

Standalones

Lies Never Sleep

Dex

Haunted

Fall into Romance

AUTHOR'S NOTE

Thanks so much for reading *Don't Forget Me*. I hope you're enjoying Alex's journey as much as I am. When I first wrote him as Macy's troublemaking little brother in *Gone*, I never anticipated giving him his own series! But the kid grew on me, endearing me and never quite letting go, and this continues through this series. I wasn't sure what to expect from these books when I wrote *Girl in Trouble*. He and the other characters have taken me on some twists and turns that I didn't expect (I can make plans, but the characters tend to do what *they* want!) and I'm really excited to see where it continues to go. I have my thoughts, but we'll see what Alex, Nick, and the others have to say about that!

I'd love to hear from you. The easiest way to do that is to join my mailing list (link below) and reply to any of the emails.

Anyway, if you enjoyed this book, please consider leaving a review wherever you purchased it. Not only will your review help me to better understand what you like—so I can give you more of it!—but it will also help other readers find my work. Reviews can be short—just share your honest thoughts. That's it.

AUTHOR'S NOTE

Want to know when I have a new release? Sign up here for new release updates. You'll also get a free book!

Thank you for your support! I really appreciate it—and you guys!

ABOUT THE AUTHOR

Stacy Claflin is a USA Today bestselling author who writes about complex women overcoming incredible odds. Whether it's her Gone saga of psychological thrillers, her various paranormal romance tales, or her sweet romance series, Stacy's three-dimensional characters shine through.

Decades after she wrote her first stories on construction paper and years after typing on an inherited green screen computer that weighed half a ton, Stacy realized her dream of becoming a full-time bestselling author.

When she's not busy writing or educating her kids from home, Stacy enjoys watching TV shows like Reign, Supernatural, Pretty Little Liars, and Once Upon a Time.

For more information:
stacyclaflin.com/about

Printed in Great Britain
by Amazon